CRITICS LOVE LAU

"Check out *ttyl* . . . the latest innovatic

"Myracle captures the banter and sho.
teens will enjoy the novelty of its style." —*VOYA*

"Certain appeal . . . there will certainly be an audience of teenage girls for this." —*Kliatt*

★ "Offers readers some meaty—and genuine—issues. Both revealing and innovative, this novel will inspire teens to pass it on to their friends . . ." —*School Library Journal*

"A surprisingly poignant tale of friendship, change and growth." —*Kirkus Reviews*

"True to the style of teen communications." —Teenreads.com

READERS LOVE LAUREN MYRACLE'S *ttyl*

"I just started reading *ttyl* and it's really cool! I hope you will write more books in IM form because my friends and I looooove to IM!!!" —Taylor

"hey! i finished *ttyl* last night, 😢 it was such a good book but now i can't read it anymore!! 😞 " —Madison

"I recently read your book *ttyl*. It is now one of my all time favorite books ever! I loved the way it was all written in Instant Messaging. It reminded me a whole lot about myself—from the crazy and fun things my friends and I talk about on IM to all the drama we talk about." —Kayla

"*ttyl* rocks my socks off! A few days ago I visited a small bookstore and was looking around knowing that I wouldn't find anything and probably would buy a book and only read the 1st like 3 pages and not know what the heck was going on! But, when I was looking around, a book titled *ttyl* caught my eye (IM SO GLAD IT DID) . . . I started reading the first pages and was like wow this is really cool and I purchased the book and was reading it on the way home and before I knew it I was up every night until like 1:30 AM just reading your book!" —Sophie

Other books by Lauren Myracle

Also in the *Internet Girls* series
ttfn
l8r, g8r

Rhymes with Witches
Kissing Kate
Eleven
Twelve

ttyl

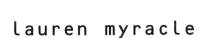

lauren myracle

Amulet Books
New York

The Library of Congress has cataloged the hardcover edition as follows:
Myracle, Lauren, 1969–
  Ttyl / Lauren Myracle.
      p. cm.
Summary: Chronicles, in "instant message" format, the day-to-day experiences, feelings, and plans of three friends, Zoe, Maddie, and Angela, as they begin tenth grade.
hardcover ISBN 10: 0-8109-4821-4
hardcover ISBN 13: 978-0-8109-4821-1
[1. Instant messaging—Fiction. 2. Friendship—Fiction. 3. Interpersonal relations—Fiction. 4. High schools—Fiction. 5. Schools—Fiction.] I. Title: Talk to you later. II. Title.
PZ7.M9955Tt 2004
[Fic]—dc22
2003016280
paperback ISBN 13: 978-0-8109-8788-3
paperback ISBN 10: 0-8109-8788-0

First published by Amulet Books in 2004.

Copyright © 2004 Lauren Myracle

Printed and bound in U.S.A.
20 19 18 17 16 15 14 13 12

Design: Interrobang Design Studio

HNA
harry n. abrams, inc.
a subsidiary of La Martinière Groupe
115 West 18th Street
New York, NY 10011
www.hnabooks.com

For the Beer Bros, of course. Cheers!

Acknowledgments

Thanks to my informants—er, *consultants*—Sarah Chesney and Laura Chaddock, for helping me with the form. Thanks to Jack, Laura, Suzy, Julianne, Mag, and Gin for giving me great advice on the story itself. And finally, a special Angela-style thank you to my editor, Susan Van Metre, whose idea this novel was in the first place: Wh-hoo! We did it! *SUPERFLYINGTACKLE-POUNCE*

SnowAngel: hey, mads! 1st day of 10th grade down the tube—wh-hoo!

mad maddie: hiyas, angela. wh-hoo to u 2.

SnowAngel: did u get the daisy i put in your locker?

mad maddie: i did

mad maddie: what's the story?

SnowAngel: i just know that the end of the summer always throws u into a funk, so i wanted to do something to defunkify u.

mad maddie: u wanted to DEFUNKIFY me?

SnowAngel: so that's why i gave u the daisy, to remind u of picnics and hanging out at the pool and going to tuckaway with zoe's parents. happy, smiley, daisy kinda stuff, u know?

mad maddie: oh. well, thanks.

SnowAngel: cuz even tho school's started, nothing has to change. u, me, and zoe—we're gonna have a great year. 😁

mad maddie: r we?

mad maddie: god, i'm already depressed just from watching everyone compare tans.

SnowAngel: why did that depress u? ur brown as a berry.

mad maddie: all day long there was far 2 much squealing going on, 2 much "ooo, u look fabulous!" and "it's so good to c u!"

SnowAngel: but why is that bad?

mad maddie: cuz it's so fake. all that clique stuff, i hate it. i hate feeling like everyone knows the secret handshake but me.

1

SnowAngel:	well, at least u and zoe r in the same homeroom. i am insanely jealous. *shakes fist at sky*
mad maddie:	**i'll c u in math, tho. whoopee.**
SnowAngel:	and thank god all 3 of us have the same lunch period. *raises champagne glass* TO THE WINSOME THREESOME! BFF!
mad maddie:	**cheers**
SnowAngel:	anyway, it doesn't matter how many secret handshakes pop up, cuz we'll always have each other. unlike susie smith—did u hear? all summer she hung out with catherine and leigh at the piedmont driving club, but now that school's started, leigh and catherine have totally dumped her.
mad maddie:	**what a pisser. susie must be heartbroken.**
SnowAngel:	come on, it would suck to have your friends drop u like that. leigh has a blog on grrl.com, and supposedly she posted an entire entry about how susie needs to shave her pubes. isn't that awful?
mad maddie:	**have u read it?**
SnowAngel:	not yet, but i will
mad maddie:	**my brother's new girlfriend doesn't shave her pits OR her pubes. he brought her to this family party at lake lanier last weekend, and she wore a bikini.**
SnowAngel:	that's sick
mad maddie:	**it was basically like she had a pelt. the pops pulled me aside and said in this really loud whisper, "guess she forgot to mow the lawn, huh?"**
SnowAngel:	SICK!!!
mad maddie:	**he was drunk, of course**

Send   Cancel

2

SnowAngel:	i could NEVER not shave my pubes. that is just gross. but even if i did have a pubic hair problem, which i do not, u and zoe would still luv me, right?
mad maddie:	**hmm . . .**
SnowAngel:	i just mean we would never turn on each other for something stupid.
mad maddie:	**no, just for something un-stupid.**
SnowAngel:	maddie! i'm serious. ppl always say that high school friendships don't last, but we're gonna prove them wrong.
mad maddie:	**right on, sister**
SnowAngel:	remember the 1st day of junior high, when we all got put in the same PE class? and we had to do that retarded president's fitness dealie, and ms. cahill made me do the stationary arm hang even tho i told her i totally couldn't?
mad maddie:	**that wasn't on the 1st day. that was like a month into the semester.**
SnowAngel:	and my arms gave out before she counted to 3. it was so humiliating. and everybody laffed except u and zoe.
mad maddie:	**cuz we are true blue**
SnowAngel:	that's right. and we'll STAY true blue 4ever and ever. we'll all 3 go to the same college and fall in luv with awesome guys who r also best friends, and we'll be bridesmaids in each other's weddings and live happily ever after. *sigh*
mad maddie:	**whatevs. but i'm not wearing pink, even for u.**
mad maddie:	**hey, g2g. the moms is yelling her head off for me to come to dinner.**

Send   Cancel

3

SnowAngel:	first u have to say it: maddie, angela, and zoe— together 4ever!
mad maddie:	**er, maddie, angela, and zoe . . . what was that last part?**
SnowAngel:	*glares*
mad maddie:	**i'm kidding, i'm kidding. but i don't HAVE to say it, angela, cuz it's true no matter what. don't make me get all mushy.**
SnowAngel:	atta girl, mads. c u tomorrow!

Tuesday, September 7, 6:01 PM

zoegirl:	angela, thank u for the daisy!!! that was SO sweet.
SnowAngel:	zoe! u found it—yay!
zoegirl:	i was all overwhelmed with first day madness, and then i opened my locker, and voila!
SnowAngel:	i gave one to maddie 2. they're to remind us not to get caught up in stupid school stuff. we've just got to be ourselves and have as much fun as possible. 😊
zoegirl:	well, it totally made me smile.
SnowAngel:	a fabulous start to a fabulous year. and it is gonna be fabulous—i can feel it. i'm gonna meet the boy of my dreams, maddie's gonna stop being so down on herself all the time, and ur gonna . . . huh. what r u gonna do? ur already perfect.
zoegirl:	what?!! hardly
SnowAngel:	ok, then what's your goal for sophomore year? AND DON'T SAY STRAIGHT "A"S, CUZ I'M NOT TALKING ABOUT SCHOOL.
zoegirl:	my goal?
zoegirl:	i have no idea

Send   Cancel

SnowAngel:	well, think of something
zoegirl:	i guess . . . i guess i just want something meaningful to happen. something BIG. my life is so boring compared to yours and maddie's. for once i want something exciting to happen, and i wanna be the one it happens to.
SnowAngel:	yeah, baby. i can groove to that.
SnowAngel:	but u'll have to MAKE it happen. u can't just sit back and be good little zoe like u usually r.
zoegirl:	well, right, that's my point. i wanna STOP being good little zoe. i wanna try out whatever comes along.
SnowAngel:	excellent plan, just as long as it doesn't involve the sit 'n' snip. promise?
zoegirl:	freak. your haircut looks great.
SnowAngel:	right. i hate my hair! ☹ even my mom was like, "well it's not the most flattering cut u've ever had, but it'll grow out."
SnowAngel:	i always get these grand ideas of "oh, this style will be perfect," and then afterward, all i wanna do is go back in time to the good ol' days of ponytails and braids. but noooooo, it's 2 late, and now i'm in clippie hell til it grows out.
zoegirl:	please. u couldn't look bad if u tried.
SnowAngel:	if i wore a t-shirt that said, "i got my hair cut at sit 'n' snip," i'd put them out of business in an hour.
zoegirl:	angela, angela, angela. do u remember last year when u henna-ed your hair? only mary kate thought u said hint a', like just a hint a' red, not 2 much and not 2 little? and she went to walmart to buy some and was SO bummed when they didn't have any?

SnowAngel:	your point would be. . . ?
zoegirl:	that even tho u hated your henna look, everyone else wanted to steal it for their own. mary kate's gonna show up tomorrow in a jillion clippies, just wait n c.
SnowAngel:	god, ur full of it.
zoegirl:	so hey, i'm outta here. i've got to read 3 chapters of The Great Gatsby by tomorrow.
SnowAngel:	the horror!
zoegirl:	thanks again for the daisy. bye!!!

Wednesday, September 8, 8:14 PM

SnowAngel:	hey, zoe!
zoegirl:	hi, angela. how r ya?
SnowAngel:	ooo, i am good. wanna know why?
SnowAngel:	cuz—drumroll, please—ROB TYLER is in my french class!!! *breathes deeply, with hand to throbbing bosom* on friday we have to do "une dialogue" together. i get to ask for a bite of his hot dog.
zoegirl:	u do not
SnowAngel:	yes, and it will be tres sexy. he is SO cute, zoe. today he was wearing this yellow button-down that was quite unexpected on a retro boy like him. he had the sleeves rolled up, and i'm telling u, he's got the greatest forearms.
zoegirl:	does he, now?
SnowAngel:	it's from doing construction work all summer. isn't that cool that he worked construction? it's so . . . manly.

Send   Cancel

zoegirl:	sounds like u guys actually talked.
SnowAngel:	our seats r right next to each other. and tonite when i do my homework, i get to fantasize about his summer sausage. *nudge, nudge, wink, wink*
zoegirl:	great, while i'll be reading 5000 pages of The Great Gatsby and answering probing discussion questions about the american dream. mr. h expects us to read a book a week. can u believe that?
SnowAngel:	like that'll be a problem for u.
SnowAngel:	did he stare at your boobs?
zoegirl:	who, mr. h?
SnowAngel:	maddie and i had him for journalism last year, and he was always staring at some girl's boobs, mostly maddie's. he was always "reading" her shirts.
zoegirl:	ewww!
SnowAngel:	so watch out. he makes a big deal of being all Christian, but what that MEANS is that he's majorly sexually repressed. whereas i, on the other hand, am not sexually repressed at all. speaking of, better start practicing for rob. bye!

Wednesday, September 8, 8:33 PM

SnowAngel:	me again. turn on the WB—that old navy commercial is on! I AM IN LUV WITH MR. BOOT CUT! *struts about to funky big band music*
zoegirl:	i thought u were in love with rob!
SnowAngel:	hey, there's plenty of me to go around. ☺ bye!

Send   Cancel

Wednesday, September 8, 9:21 PM

mad maddie: **hola, zoe**

zoegirl: hey, mads

mad maddie: **well, i hear angela's selected her first crush of the season.**

zoegirl: rob tyler? or mr. boot cut?

mad maddie: **she's so funny. it's like she's got to have a guy to like, or she can't exist. it drives me batty.**

zoegirl: yeah, well, that's angela

zoegirl: so is rob worthy? i've never had a class with him.

mad maddie: **i guess he's nice enuff, in a slouchy, hipster-boy kinda way. but i must say, he's got a weak chin.**

zoegirl: oh, man! he kinda does!

mad maddie: **i know angela thinks he's hot, but he reminds me of david spade. NOT a good thing.**

zoegirl: think he'll fall for her?

mad maddie: **they always do, don't they?**

zoegirl: but then things never end up working out. why is that, do u think?

mad maddie: **because every new guy is, like, a god to her. she puts them on this total pedestal, and then they do something crappy and she falls apart. and WE have to pick up the pieces.**

zoegirl: well let's not forget the time u fell deeply and madly in luv with grier snelling, shall we?

mad maddie: **hold on, now—i was in the 7th grade!!!**

zoegirl: and u sent him that perfumed letter for v-day, only u were 2 chicken to put your name on it, and he was like, "ew, my desk stinks! ew, who put this here?!"

Send   Cancel

mad maddie:	**thanks for bringing up such a joyous memory. i was scarred for life, thank u very much.**
zoegirl:	but angela and i put u back together, because that's what friends do. and if we have to, u and i will do the same for her.
zoegirl:	anyway, maybe this time'll be different.
mad maddie:	**and maybe the pope will fly. l8rs, chickie!**

Thursday, September 9, 7:46 PM

mad maddie:	**hey, angela. i'm glad ur here, because i am SOOOO pissed.**
SnowAngel:	oh, no! why?
mad maddie:	**1 word. well, 2. JANA WHITAKER.**
SnowAngel:	the queen bee? *gasps in shock* what'd she do this time?
mad maddie:	**i hate her. she's evil.**
SnowAngel:	i KNOW that. TELL ME WHAT SHE DID!!!!
mad maddie:	**fine. we had a substitute for last period study hall and he insisted on taking roll, cuz god forbid one of us had snuck off to do something productive. when he got to me he called out, "madeleine kinnick?" and jana turns around, all batting eyes and innocent, and goes, "um, isn't your name madigan?"**
SnowAngel:	but your name IS madigan.
mad maddie:	**yeah, which jana totally knows!**
SnowAngel:	so what's the problem?
mad maddie:	**r u serious?!!**
mad maddie:	**it was the way she said it, like she was honestly confused. like, "oh my goodness, i THINK i know u, don't i?" WHEN WE'VE GONE TO SCHOOL TOGETHER SINCE 7th GRADE!!!**

Send   Cancel

9

SnowAngel: ooooo, i can c how that would be annoying.

mad maddie: **it's like she thinks she's so much better than all the rest of us, and she's doing us a favor if she remembers our names. god. it bugs the hell out of me how she walks down the halls in her gauzy skirts and peasant blouses, her belly button ring shouting, "look how cool i am! worship me! adore me!" as if she's such a rebel just cuz she pierced her navel.**

SnowAngel: so true. margie walker pierces her navel, and everyone writes her off as a sk8r punk cuz she happens to have blue hair. but jana whitaker pierces her navel, and she's Funky Alternative Girl. so brave! so risque! let's all run out and copy her so we can be little jana clones!

mad maddie: **i know. it's pathetic.**

SnowAngel: anyway, jana's totally backstabbing margaret cheney. did u know that?

mad maddie: **exsqueeze me?**

SnowAngel: it almost makes me feel sorry for margaret, cuz she and jana r supposed to be best buds. but i guess it's margaret's own fault for ever trusting jana in the first place.

mad maddie: **explain**

SnowAngel: well, i was in the bathroom after 5th period, right? and jana and terri were there, and jana was going on about what a bitch margaret was for flirting with rex saunders. i guess rex is like jana's property cuz they went to some party together over the summer. jana was all, "she is such a whore," and then she lowered her voice like she was telling some big secret and said something REALLY gross.

Send   Cancel

mad maddie:	**and that would be . . . ?**
SnowAngel:	omg
SnowAngel:	well, she said that margaret . . . er . . . ejaculates.
mad maddie:	**WHAT?!!!**
SnowAngel:	well, actually she said she squirts when she comes. and then she was like, "shit, i can't believe i told u. u've gotta swear not to tell, terri. u've gotta swear!" while the whole time i was 2 sinks over going, "HELLO! do u even know i'm here?"
mad maddie:	**that is disgusting**
SnowAngel:	i know. i was like, "margaret is your friend, u asshole. how would u like it if she went around spreading rumors about u?"
mad maddie:	**i meant the other part. about margaret.**
SnowAngel:	oh. well, yeah.
SnowAngel:	some girls really do, tho. i read it in our bodies, ourselves.
mad maddie:	**ick**
mad maddie:	**but . . . does jana truly NOT know my name? is that possible?**
SnowAngel:	if so, it's her loss.
mad maddie:	**it just made me feel so loser-ish. christine and amber giggled when she said it, and i wanted to crawl under my desk. not that they would have noticed, since to them i'm totally invisible.**
SnowAngel:	ur not invisible, maddie. not to the ppl who matter. hey! *lightbulb binging in head* want me to bring u some krispy kremes to cheer u up?
mad maddie:	**YEAH!**

Send   Cancel

11

SnowAngel:	ok, only i'll have to wait for mom to get back so she can give me a ride.
mad maddie:	**never mind. by then i'll probly have killed myself. lol**
SnowAngel:	poor sad maddie. i can't wait til we get our licenses. then we can do stuff like that whenever we want.
mad maddie:	**4 weeks and a day, baby. now if only i could get the moms to buy me that jeep . . .**
SnowAngel:	dream on. maybe your grandmom's old gremlin . . .
mad maddie:	**the gremlin OWNS. it runs, anywayz.**
mad maddie:	**hey, wanna hear my post-driving-test fantasy?**
SnowAngel:	er . . . i dunno. do i?
mad maddie:	**i know it's probably totally impossible, but wouldn't it be awesome if u, me, and zoe could go on a road trip together, just the 3 of us?**
SnowAngel:	omg, that would be so cool.
mad maddie:	**crank up the music, roll down the windows, and just GO.**
SnowAngel:	we could drive to tuckaway. or hilton head! we could be beach blanket bimbos! 😎
mad maddie:	**and we could get away from everything having to do with school. we could just leave it all behind us.**
SnowAngel:	aw, man. that would be so awesome.
SnowAngel:	SHIT, maddie, why do u put these ideas in my head? now i totally wanna do it!
mad maddie:	**but the rents will never let us. well, mine would if i begged hard enuff, cuz they don't give a shit what i do. but yours and zoe's would freak out.**
SnowAngel:	i know. that so sucks.
mad maddie:	**1 day, tho . . .**

Send   Cancel

SnowAngel:	well, i call shotgun on our first krispy kreme run.
mad maddie:	**u got it. byeas!**

Thursday, September 9, 8:25 PM

SnowAngel:	hey, zo. maddie told me what happened in study hall. was jana really out to humiliate her, or is maddie just being dramatic?
zoegirl:	maddie? dramatic? hahahahaha
SnowAngel:	but did jana really say all that, like jana didn't even know maddie's name?
zoegirl:	yeah, only . . . i don't know. i think jana just wanted to straighten out the sub without technically correcting him.
SnowAngel:	oh
zoegirl:	don't tell maddie i said that, tho. she gets so weird when it comes to jana and that crowd.
SnowAngel:	it's that whole stupid in-crowd thing. it's so not fair. the nice ppl—like US—should be the popular ones. then we'd have all the power, but we'd use it in a good way. like if jana made some snide remark about someone's kmart clothes, we could bitch-slap her til she apologized.
zoegirl:	oh definitely. me, the bitch-slapper.
SnowAngel:	and the next time she slammed someone's reputation—remember when she "let it slip" about heidi larson's shoplifting charge?—we could dig up some dirt on her and post it on principal eddie's web page. then she'd know what it felt like.
zoegirl:	uh-huh

zoegirl:	listen, i've got a conference with mr. h tomorrow, and i'm supposed to make a list of possible essay topics. it's my 1st big assignment, and my mom is already on my back about it. so i've g2g, ok?
SnowAngel:	enjoy!

Thursday, September 9, 9:05 PM

mad maddie:	**did they say anything else?**
SnowAngel:	who?
mad maddie:	**jana and terri, when u were in the bathroom with them.**
SnowAngel:	no, except jana did mention how excited she was to be in homeroom with madeleine kinnick. JK!!!!
mad maddie:	**ur a laff riot**
SnowAngel:	i know ☺
SnowAngel:	seriously, maddie, jana is SO not worth your time. stop letting it get to u.
mad maddie:	**ur right. byeas!**

Friday, September 10, 8:51 PM

mad maddie:	**hiyas, zo. how was your meeting with mr. h?**
zoegirl:	it was good. it was kinda cool, actually, cuz after we talked about my paper, we talked about religion and stuff.
mad maddie:	**in other words he stared at your boobs and lectured u about the sins of the body?**
zoegirl:	no, that's not at all what happened.
mad maddie:	**when i had him for journalism last year, he was always having girls stay late for "conferences." once he made jody fisher stay late and he went off on her about her**

Send   Cancel

	tongue ring, like why exactly did she get it done and had she heard of the WAIT plan and shit like that.
zoegirl:	i have a really hard time believing that.
zoegirl:	or if he did say something, he was probably just trying to watch out for her. like he didn't want her to get herpes of the mouth or anything.
mad maddie:	**she said he got a total stiffie while they were talking. she said it was hysterical.**
zoegirl:	that's ridiculous. mr. h would never do that.
mad maddie:	**what makes u so sure?**
zoegirl:	cuz he's NICE. cuz he treated me like i was a person instead of a kid. that's what was so great—we were just 2 ppl having a discussion.
mad maddie:	**ohhhh. so what did the 2 of u "discuss"?**
zoegirl:	NOT tongue rings or anything like that. geez. we both said how we believe there's meaning to life, that everything's not random and pointless like some ppl think. and mr. h talked about Christianity a little—how he's sure God has a plan for him. he told me that everything that happens, happens for a reason. doesn't that give u the chills?
mad maddie:	**yesterday at publix, a little kid rammed me with a grocery cart. was there a message there? cuz i think i missed it.**
zoegirl:	he also said that sometimes u'll meet someone totally unexpected and it'll change your life in a way u can't even imagine. now that really gave me the chills.
mad maddie:	**zoe. do u even hear what ur saying?**
zoegirl:	what?

Send   Cancel

15

mad maddie:	**"it'll change your life in a way u can't even imagine"? he is so hitting on u!!!**
zoegirl:	shut up. just cuz u can't be serious, that doesn't mean no one else can.
zoegirl:	it was a good convo. it felt . . . important.
mad maddie:	**whatevs. i still say he's hitting on u.**
zoegirl:	i'm outta here. bye!!!

Friday, September 10, 9:19 PM

mad maddie:	**i just put on godsmack in your honor. thought u should know.**
zoegirl:	rotflmao
mad maddie:	**it's giving me the chills, baby.**
zoegirl:	GOOD-BYE!

Sunday, September 12, 8:52 PM

SnowAngel:	aarrghhh! 🙁
zoegirl:	well, hello to u 2.
SnowAngel:	aarrghhhhhhh!
zoegirl:	something bothering u?
SnowAngel:	chrissy dropped my face brush into the toilet!!!
zoegirl:	huh?
SnowAngel:	my hinoki polishing facial brush—IN THE TOILET!!! *stomps on picture of chrissy*
zoegirl:	u brush your face?
SnowAngel:	u r missing the point. my sister dropped my face brush into the toilet, which was, yes, currently in use. by HER. AND she's got strep,

Send   Cancel

	so her pee is all orange from antibiotics. *stomp stomp stomp*
zoegirl:	i take it ur not happy about this.
SnowAngel:	would u be? i use my face brush to wash my FACE. u know, instead of a washcloth. it lifts away dead cells while improving circulation.
zoegirl:	u don't say
SnowAngel:	AND I JUST THIS VERY SECOND USED IT!!!! AFTER SHE DROPPED IT IN THE FREAKIN TOILET!!!!!!!!
zoegirl:	ewww. why?
SnowAngel :	*pulls hair from roots* cuz she didn't TELL me until just now! she thought i'd be mad!
zoegirl:	so basically u washed your face in chrissy's stinky orange pee?
SnowAngel:	u r not being helpful. *stomps on picture of zoe AND picture of chrissy*
zoegirl:	i'm sorry, but that really is disgusting. surely chrissy washed it off.
SnowAngel:	she RINSED it. that's what she says, she RINSED it. like that makes me feel a hell of a lot better.
zoegirl:	back in christopher columbus's time, ppl used to brush their teeth with pee. did u know that?
SnowAngel:	*breathes deeply* i did not know that, zoe.
zoegirl:	altho i think it was only ppl who were taking long sea voyages and ran out of toothpaste . . .
SnowAngel:	that's it. good bye.
zoegirl:	wait! angela?

zoegirl:	angela!!!!
zoegirl:	fine. just don't expect me to kiss u tomorrow. air kisses, that's all u'll get!
zoegirl:	ANGELA!!!!!!

Monday, September 13, 5:15 PM

SnowAngel:	hellooo, maddie
mad maddie:	**hellooo, angela**
SnowAngel:	i saw jana whitaker after 6th period today. she was looking especially tacky in her sparkly emerald eyeshadow, and she was totally ripping on julie matthews. i swear, she is ALWAYS putting down ppl who are supposedly her friends. have u noticed?
mad maddie:	**what'd she say?**
SnowAngel:	well, terri was like, "oh, julie, u look so cute. u look just like kirsten dunst in 'crazy/beautiful.'" and jana goes, "so true! u could totally be her twin, before she got skinny." !!!
mad maddie:	**ouch**
SnowAngel:	it was so sad, cuz julie turned beet red and started tugging on her shirt, like to cover herself up or something, and jana was all, "just stick to your diet, you'll get there." as if the whole "before she got skinny" was ok since it was mixed in with this great show of support. but julie's not even that fat, so there was no reason for jana to say all that in the 1st place.
mad maddie:	**does jana have a reason for anything she says? no**
SnowAngel:	i swear, she's like an infection. she gloms on

Send   Cancel

18

	wherever she spots a weakness and makes it five thousand times worse.
mad maddie:	**and yet everyone still worships her and secretly craves her approval. why is that?**
SnowAngel:	i have NO idea. anyway, not everyone craves her approval, cuz i certainly don't. and u don't, of course.
SnowAngel:	right?
mad maddie:	**please. this morning ms. andrist got onto me about being tardy, and i could tell jana was laffing about it behind my back. i can always tell. it's like i have jana radar. so i gave her the evil eye and was like, "yeah? u want some of this, homegirl?"**
SnowAngel:	good for u, homegirl. *flicks jana off the stage*
mad maddie:	**what about u and rob? how's that going?**
SnowAngel:	oh, pah. u know how i told u that today was the day i was gonna make my move? well, he sat next to me in french, and i acted totally blase. just, "hey, rob." no real excitement in my voice or anything.
mad maddie:	**why? at lunch u were like, "watch out, bubba. here i come."**
SnowAngel:	i know, so what's my deal? i need to help him along as much as possible, or else forget about him. i get so mad at myself when i act disinterested around guys i like. 😑
mad maddie:	**yes, it's a real trauma**
SnowAngel:	it is!
SnowAngel:	oh, hold on. doug schmidt's IMing me—let me tell him something real quick.
SnowAngel:	ok, i'm back

Send   Cancel

19

mad maddie:	**what did doug want?**
SnowAngel:	to know if i wanted to go bike riding. i told him i was sick, but i don't think he believed me.
mad maddie:	**hmm, wonder why. maybe cuz u've rejected him once a week for the past 2 years?**
SnowAngel:	well, he should stop asking me!
SnowAngel:	uh-oh—now he wants to know if he should bring me some chicken soup. what should i tell him?
mad maddie:	**the truth, dammit. that he's simply not in your league and he should aim his sights lower, like at cameron diaz, for example. maybe SHE wants some chicken soup.**
SnowAngel:	maddie! *gazes at friend reproachfully* u make me sound awful.
mad maddie:	**well think about how it sounds: oh no, a guy asked me out! how terrible! and now he wants to bring me get-well gifts!**
SnowAngel:	stop it. i hate turning doug down again and again. but isn't it better to do that than to lead him on?
mad maddie:	**i suppose**
SnowAngel:	there, i told doug VERY NICELY that i don't need any soup cuz i look 2 terrible to come to the door. r u happy?
mad maddie:	**u should have told him to screw the soup and bring u ice cream instead. or a slurpee.**
SnowAngel:	be serious. AM i awful? am i shallow and self-centered cuz i don't wanna go out with doug?
mad maddie:	**yes**
SnowAngel:	god, now i'm all paranoid
SnowAngel:	hey, doug must have gotten off-line, cuz his name's

Send   Cancel

off my buddy list. maybe i'll call him just to chat so
he'll know i'm not a jerk. and then afterward i'll call
rob and turn on the ol' charm, so that he'll know i'm
NOT disinterested.

mad maddie: **ur hopeless. it's official.**

SnowAngel: g2g! bye!

Monday, September 13, 5:45 PM

SnowAngel: OMG!!!

mad maddie: **what?!**

SnowAngel: i called rob, just like i said i would, and he asked me
out! for TONITE!!!

mad maddie: **damn, girl. u r good.**

SnowAngel: i know, i know! he's taking me out to dinner, and then
we're going to some party at kyle's.

SnowAngel: hey, u could come if u want—u and zoe both! not to
the dinner part, obviously, but rob says kyle's party
is gonna be huge.

mad maddie: **kyle's having a party on a monday nite?**

SnowAngel: his parents r out of town, but they're coming back on
wednesday, so this is the only nite he can do it. u
should come!

mad maddie: **yeah, that's what i wanna do—have the moms drop me**
off at kyle's in front of the whole friggin grade. with my
luck jana would be there laffing her head off.

SnowAngel: I CAN'T BELIEVE I HAVE A DATE WITH ROB!
MUST GO PRIMP!

mad maddie: **byeas!**

Send   Cancel

Tuesday, September 14, 4:15 PM

SnowAngel: zoe, dahling!

zoegirl: u better be IMing to tell me about your madcap nite with rob. u can't put me off any longer!!!

SnowAngel: he was sitting RIGHT BEHIND US, zoe. what did u want me to do, announce to his face how in luv with him i am?

zoegirl: it was the cafeteria. it was loud. u could have said anything and he wouldn't have heard.

SnowAngel: well, if ur gonna get all sniffy about it . . .

zoegirl: **TELL ME!!!**

SnowAngel: ok. me: long-sleeve white shirt, knee-length denim skirt with flower print, wooden platform sandals, silver square bracelet, garnet ring. hair down. him: "moab" t-shirt on top of long-sleeve blue shirt, jeans, sneaks. adorable sticky-up-y hair.

zoegirl: very nice, altho i'm not sure i agree about his hair. i saw it at lunch, and i'm thinking it's more lack of hygiene than stylistic flair.

zoegirl: where'd he take u to eat?

SnowAngel: we went to bennigan's. mmmm. and while we were waiting for our food, he told this hysterical story about this time he called the home shopping network. they were selling a watch that was supposedly indestructible, and rob asked the lady, "yes, but does it resist cheese dip?" only he pronounced it really funny, like che-e-e-ese dip.

zoegirl: i wish i knew how to tell funny stories. i always get embarrassed and start mumbling, and then i wish i'd never started.

Send   Cancel

SnowAngel:	and then he said, "cuz my last watch stopped working when i dropped it in a bowl of che-e-e-ese dip. so tell me: this solid gold watch u've got on the screen there, can it handle the dairy products?
SnowAngel:	they broadcast his voice and everthing! god, i wish i'd been watching when he called in.
zoegirl:	so what'd u do after dinner?
SnowAngel:	we went to that party at kyle's and danced the nite away to patrick benson's awful garage band. well, i danced. rob kinda shifted his weight from one foot to the other.
zoegirl:	white man's boogie. did he bite his lower lip?
SnowAngel:	no, but he bit mine! 😊 l8r, that is, when he took me home. yippee! the boy can kiss!
zoegirl:	go, angela!
SnowAngel:	*sighs in ecstasy*
SnowAngel:	what about u, what's up in your world?
zoegirl:	ack. nothing nearly so exciting—altho u might wanna talk to maddie if u haven't already.
SnowAngel:	why?
zoegirl:	cuz i highly doubt she wants to talk to me.
SnowAngel:	no, i meant why should i talk to her? what happened?
zoegirl:	well, she called me up to get my opinion on this letter she'd written, and i . . . ah, crap.
SnowAngel:	what? what did u do?!
zoegirl:	i corrected her grammar
SnowAngel:	u didn't
zoegirl:	i did

Send   Cancel

SnowAngel:	zoe! u know how much she hates being corrected—especially by u!
zoegirl:	i thought i was helping!
SnowAngel:	oh, god
zoegirl:	and then i told her i was just being anal and to forget everything i'd said, and she said, "u don't have to lie, zoe."
SnowAngel:	ouch
zoegirl:	so will u talk to her?
SnowAngel:	i'll IM her right now.
zoegirl:	thanks
SnowAngel:	brb!

Tuesday, September 14, 4:33 PM

SnowAngel:	mads! wazzup?
mad maddie:	**ur interrupting a very important quiz on my planetary personality. did zoe tell u to check on me?**
SnowAngel:	???
mad maddie:	**so—hold on, my results r processing. wanna hear what planet i am?**
SnowAngel:	uh, sure
mad maddie:	**i scored 85% Powerful Pluto. here's what it says:** *Although you tend to wallow in your misery, Pluto's energy gives you the power to change your life—if you dare. It may be scary, but Pluto doesn't care. This planet knows how to play with the big boys.*
SnowAngel:	ooo, i wanna play with the big boys. send me the quiz.
mad maddie:	**i'll forward it when we get off. i'll forward it to zoe 2.**

SnowAngel:	so ur NOT mad at her. yay!
mad maddie:	**excuse me?**
SnowAngel:	oh, uh . . . *does freaky hand gestures as a distraction technique*
mad maddie:	**forget it. i don't care. she told u about my pathetic letter?**
SnowAngel:	she didn't say it was pathetic, i swear. she's worried that ur mad at her, that's all.
mad maddie:	**well, i'm not bursting with joy.**
SnowAngel:	who was the letter to, anyway? i don't get it.
mad maddie:	**well, if u MUST hear the whole sad story . . .**
SnowAngel:	i must
mad maddie:	**fine. chapter 1: maddie is in study hall with evil jana, who is writing notes to terri and laffing hysterically like ha-ha, we have a life and u don't.**
SnowAngel:	god, i hate it when ppl do that. like they're trying to rub it in your face how much fun they're having.
mad maddie:	**chapter 2: class is dismissed and everyone goes squealing out of the room. only maddie stupidly leaves her geometry notebook, and so she goes back to get it. and there, in the hall by her locker, is jana. by herself. there is no one else around, just jana and maddie. r u with me?**
SnowAngel:	uh oh . . .
mad maddie:	**chapter 3: maddie, being the kind good soul that she is, decides to say "hello." just "hello," all right? normal ppl do it all the time. AND WHAT DOES JANA DO? she keeps shoving books into her backpack, la-di-da, like no one is freakin there! she didn't even look up or nod or anything!**

Send   Cancel

25

SnowAngel: ooh, that makes me so mad. that is SO ridiculous!!!

SnowAngel: but why do u even care what jana does or doesn't do?

mad maddie: **chapter 4: maddie buys a king size snickers at 7-11 to ease her pain. chapter 5: the snickers is rotten inside. like, really, really nasty. chapter 6: maddie whips off a complaint letter in a frenzy of self-righteousness. chapter 7: maddie calls zoe and reads it to her over the phone. and chapter 8: zoe makes maddie feel like total shit, as usual, which is just lovely after a day like this.**

SnowAngel: oh, maddie 😞

mad maddie: **i was like all proud of myself, and she starts lecturing me on what a dumbass i am who can't even write a stupid complaint letter.**

SnowAngel: *tsk, tsk* she did not say u were a dumbass and u know it.

mad maddie: **i just hate it that she's so good at everything and that i suck.**

SnowAngel: did u tell her all the jana stuff? before u read your letter?

mad maddie: **no. i was already humiliated enuff, thank u very much.**

SnowAngel: but zoe wouldn't care. i mean, she'd care, but in a good way.

mad maddie: **yeah, well**

SnowAngel: anyway, maybe jana didn't hear u. maybe that's why she didn't say "hi" back.

mad maddie: **right. she didn't hear me when we were practically the only 2 ppl in the entire hall.**

SnowAngel: listen, madikins. u have to get off this "poor

Send   Cancel

pitiful me" kick cuz U R AWESOME. u want a list of all your glorious qualities?

mad maddie: **no**

mad maddie: **yes**

SnowAngel: ur funny. ur tough. u have awesome style even tho u never wear makeup. (u really SHOULD let me give u a makeover.) u can pull off the whole cargo-pants-and-a-tank look better than anyone, even kim possible, and your cheekbones r freakin incredible. even my mom says so.

mad maddie: **she does?**

SnowAngel: yeah. she's like, maddie is someone whose looks r only gonna improve as she gets older.

mad maddie: **that does not sound like a compliment**

SnowAngel: and zoe and i are both insanely jealous of your hair. ur like "lion-girl" with your tumbled golden curls.

mad maddie: **zoe is not jealous of any single part of me, even—excuse me while i gag—my "tumbled golden curls."**

SnowAngel: we LUV u, mads. i luv u and zoe luvs u, and just so u know, she really does feel bad.

mad maddie: **whatevs. it's no big deal.**

SnowAngel: so . . . ur all right?

mad maddie: **yeah, i'm fine.**

SnowAngel: ok, guess i'll go, then. remember, ur awesome!!!

Tuesday, September 14, 4:41 PM

SnowAngel: i'm ba-a-ck

zoegirl: hold on, mary kate just IMed me to get the english hw

27

ttyl

zoegirl:	ok, done. did u talk to maddie?
SnowAngel:	yes, and her bad mood wasn't really about u. i mean, there was the normal "zoe is so much better than me" baloney, but there was all this jana stuff going on 2. so it was like the totally wrong time for u to be a grammar nazi, but there's no way u could have known.
zoegirl:	eeesh
SnowAngel:	but anyway, she's fine.
zoegirl:	well, good. maybe now i can stop worrying about her and start focusing on my english paper. i've got another meeting with mr. h tomorrow, and i'm kinda freakin. i really wanna impress him.
SnowAngel:	no sweat. just wear a tight shirt and he'll give u an A.
zoegirl:	wanna lend me one of yours?
SnowAngel:	sure! 👍
zoegirl:	i was KIDDING, angela.
SnowAngel:	hey, if u've got it, flaunt it. that's what my mom says.
zoegirl:	that's sick
SnowAngel:	that's my mom! ttfn!

Wednesday, September 15, 7:32 PM

SnowAngel:	hey, mads. i just had a total Zoe's Scary Mother flashback.
mad maddie:	**oh yeah? spill**
SnowAngel:	well i called zoe 2 minutes ago and accidentally INTERRUPTED THEIR DINNER. *horror movie sound effects* mrs. barrett was like, "this is not an appropriate time to call, angela." it was this tiny little

Send   Cancel

28

incident, right? but i could tell she was annoyed, and it reminded me of that time zoe was supposed to meet her at starbucks but didn't. do u remember?

mad maddie: **kinda, but not really**

SnowAngel: zoe came home with me from school, and later she was supposed to meet her mom at the peachtree battle starbucks. but by 6 it was storming like crazy, and my mom was like, "no, zoe, u can't walk to starbucks in this weather. call your mom and tell her to pick u up here. she'll understand." so zoe did, and her mom came to get her. but she was PISSED.

mad maddie: **what did she do?**

SnowAngel: she was all, "u have made me go out of my way and u have wasted my time. i expect better than this from u!"

mad maddie: **sounds just like her**

SnowAngel: and my mom tried to step in and explain, and mrs. barrett totally ignored her. she just yanked zoe out of the house, and by then zoe was trying not to cry, and it was AWFUL.

mad maddie: **i try not to deal with mrs. barrett unless i absolutely have to. i don't call zoe if it's anywhere NEAR dinner time, cuz she's given me her little lecture 2.**

mad maddie: **u think that's why zoe gets so uptight sometimes? cuz her mom is always riding her?**

SnowAngel: well, duh. she thinks she has to be perfect cuz that's basically what her mom tells her every minute of the day. thank god she has us, u know?

mad maddie: **damn straight**

Send   Cancel

29

SnowAngel:	ok. breathe. *assumes zen-like posture* soon i'll be watching "that 70s show" and mrs. barrett will be a distant, hazy memory.
mad maddie:	**that's right. just let it all go.**
SnowAngel:	on a pleasanter subject, i finally took that "what planet r u" quiz. wanna hear my results?
mad maddie:	**let's have 'em**
SnowAngel:	*You scored 95% Vivacious Venus. Venus is the planet of love and pleasure, and you're the poster child. You're quite the social butterfly, and few can resist your seductive moves. You rarely deny yourself any of life's pleasures, but be careful that you don't forget the benefits of hard work and self-discipline!*
mad maddie:	**hmmm. u? a social butterfly?**
SnowAngel:	let's not leave out my seductive moves. ☺ speaking of, i'm meeting rob at 7-11 tomorrow after school. wanna come? *slips on sock puppets and sings out loud* *i love this place, my slurpee is so green!*
mad maddie:	**no thanks**
SnowAngel:	hey, zoe just popped up on my buddy list.

mad maddie:	**mine 2**	**Wednesday, September 15, 7:49 PM**
SnowAngel:	hold on—i'm gonna check in with her real quick.	
		SnowAngel: hey, zo!
SnowAngel:	so r things ok b/w u? that's 1 of the things i wanted to ask her before i got scolded.	zoegirl: hey, angela. sorry about my mom.
		SnowAngel: no problem— sorry i called during dinner.

30

mad maddie:	**i guess. after u left she kept going on and on about what a great writer i was, how i should totally send that letter. i was like, shut up, ok? i'm over it!**	hey, i'm talking to the mads 2. she says things are good between u. yay!
		zoegirl: really? god, i'm so glad. i thought maybe i'd pissed her off again.
SnowAngel:	well, u know zoe. she hates it when she thinks she's messed up.	
		SnowAngel: nah, i wouldn't worry about it.
SnowAngel:	bye, mads! time for my show! (don't tell zo what i said about her mom—duh!)	SnowAngel: so anyway, i gotta go but u can talk to maddie instead!
mad maddie:	**say hi to fez for me!**	zoegirl: ok

Wednesday, September 15, 7:55 PM

mad maddie: **hey, zo!**

zoegirl: hey, mads!

mad maddie: **i think it's just the 2 of us now.**

zoegirl: yep

mad maddie: so how'd things go with mr. h? did he hit on u again?

zoegirl: oh, please

mad maddie: **well, did u have any Deep Discussions? did he change the course of your life in a way u couldn't even imagine?**

zoegirl: not exactly . . . altho he did invite me to come to wellspring on friday.

mad maddie:	**wtf???**
zoegirl:	u know. it's a church group, only not for one particular church. it's for high school kids, and there's a devotional and singing and stuff like that. on fridays they meet for breakfast, and mr. h invited me to come.
mad maddie:	**i know what it IS, zoe. what did u say?**
zoegirl:	i said sure
mad maddie:	**u did not**
zoegirl:	did 2. he's gonna pick me up at 7 on friday morning.
mad maddie:	**zoe!!! oh, god. somebody's gonna read that poem about the footprints, i can c it now. where some guy is walking on a cliff and there's like 2 sets of footprints? and then the guy gets to a really steep part, and when he looks back one of the sets is gone? and he goes, "oh, my father, why did u forsake me in my time of need?" and God says, "oh no, my son. no, no, no. i was carrying u, don't u c?"**
zoegirl:	my grandmom has a copy of that poem in her bedroom. it's in a big gold frame.
mad maddie:	**i can't believe u said yes. i truly can't believe it.**
zoegirl:	maddie, ur overreacting. i'm just psyched mr. h asked me, and i wish u could be happy for me instead of all weird.
zoegirl:	i mean, out of all the ppl at school, he picked me. it made me feel special.
mad maddie:	**i thought u said lots of kids went to this shindig.**
zoegirl:	yeah, but i'm the only one he's giving a ride to.
mad maddie:	**whatevs. just PLEASE don't get in a back scratching train. my brother went to this lock-in once at his friend's church, and he said that all nite long everyone gave each other back scratches.**

Send   Cancel

zoegirl:	i so can't c your brother at a lock-in. mark went to a lock-in?
mad maddie:	**this was like 5000 years ago. he said back-scratching trains r how christian boys cop a feel.**
zoegirl:	relax, i won't get in a back scratching train.
mad maddie:	**all right, then. u take that quiz i sent u?**
zoegirl:	u and your quizzes. and u make fun of me for going to wellspring!
mad maddie:	**yeah, but at least with the quizzes there's nothing fishy going on. i know how full of crap they r. i just like them anywayz. so did u?**
zoegirl:	hold on, i'll pull up my results
zoegirl:	*You scored 75% Structured Saturn. Saturn is the planet of responsibility and discipline, and you couldn't be more reliable if you tried. While it's admirable to be so diligent and self-disciplined, know that life's too short not to break the rules every once in a while.*
mad maddie:	**ha! that is SO u.**
zoegirl:	thanks a lot. u and angela get the fun planets, and what do i get? i get sucky saturn, planet of responsibility and discipline.
mad maddie:	**hey, they call 'em as they c 'em.**
zoegirl:	and who would "they" be, the planetary fairies?
mad maddie:	**as opposed to the God and baby jesus fairies? jk. i really do believe in God, just not wellspring.**
zoegirl:	whatever. bye, powerful pluto.
mad maddie:	**byeas, structured saturn.**
zoegirl:	ttyl!

Wednesday, September 15, 8:40 PM

mad maddie:	**yo, angela! turn off the damn tv!**
SnowAngel:	u again! wazzup?
mad maddie:	**have u heard about zoe and mr. h? she's going with him to some sing-along this friday!**
SnowAngel:	friday morning fellowship. yeah, she told me.
mad maddie:	**they're all gonna join hands and sing "It Only Takes a Spark."**
SnowAngel:	ooo, i like that song. it makes me feel all warm inside.☺
mad maddie:	**oh god**
SnowAngel:	*looks soulfully into the distance* *that's how it is with God's love, once u experience it. u wanna sing, it's fresh like spring, u wa-a-a-nt to pas-s-s-ss it on.*
SnowAngel:	i think it's called "pass it on," come to think of it.
mad maddie:	**it just surprises me that zoe's getting all religious. i thought she was smarter than that.**
SnowAngel:	what, smart ppl can't be religious?
mad maddie:	**yeah . . . but friday morning fellowship? it's ridiculous. cherryl ann booth goes to that, wearing her little pinafores. and scott kincaid, the guy who makes those fellowship of christian athlete announcements and then prays for god's help in kicking northside's ass. zoe doesn't belong with that crowd.**
SnowAngel:	oh, phooey. maybe she'll meet some guys.
mad maddie:	**like mr. h, u mean? this is bad, angela. bad, bad, bad.**
SnowAngel:	mr. h, as in an illicit classroom romance? ooo, i never thought of it like that.
mad maddie:	**i'm serious**

Send   Cancel

SnowAngel:	me 2. it would be like in "boston public" when that really cute girl got down and dirty with her scurvy shakespeare teacher. it would be awesome.
mad maddie:	**it wouldn't be awesome. it would be disgusting.**
mad maddie:	**a teacher shouldn't be offering rides to his students when it's just going to be the 2 of them. especially when it's mr. h.**
SnowAngel:	relax, maddie. repeat after me: "zoe is just going to friday morning fellowship. she has not sold her soul to the devil."
mad maddie:	**yeah? just u wait.**
SnowAngel:	c ya!

Thursday, September 16, 5:02 PM

SnowAngel:	hiya, zoe
zoegirl:	hey, angela. i called your cell about an hour ago—did u get my message?
SnowAngel:	yeah, sorry i didn't pick up. i was hanging out with rob, just fooling around. *drools* and actually, i can't be on-line for long. he's picking me up at 8 to go hear this band at the dark horse.
zoegirl:	the dark horse? isn't that a bar?
SnowAngel:	i'm gonna use his sister's i.d.
zoegirl:	u better be careful, angela. u could get so busted if the bouncer doesn't go for it.
SnowAngel:	rob says they'd just take lisa's license and cut it up, but that's not gonna happen. so what'd u call about?
zoegirl:	well. u know i'm going to friday morning fellowship, right?

ttyl	

SnowAngel: yeah, and maddie's steamed like a potsticker.

SnowAngel: why is that, do u think? it's not like anyone's making HER go.

zoegirl: i know. it's bizarre. it's like she thinks i'm joining some beardy-weirdy religious cult.

SnowAngel: no, she's afraid ur gonna jump in the sack with mr. h.

zoegirl: angela!!! please don't even SAY that. god, like mr. h would even consider it.

SnowAngel: would u want him to?

zoegirl: very funny. anyway, i think it has to do with the whole religious thing, and the fact that i'm hanging out with new ppl. all day at school maddie called me her sister in christ, and then she'd throw out a word like "shit" or "balls" and gasp as if she was afraid she'd offended me. "oh dear," she'd say. "will your new friends be pissed? i mean, perturbed?"

SnowAngel: she's just teasing

zoegirl: yeah, but it's so irritating. i wouldn't care if she wanted to hang out with other ppl.

SnowAngel: r u kidding? i would! 4ever friends, remember? the winsome threesome?

zoegirl: yeah, but that doesn't mean JUST us.

SnowAngel: it doesn't? jk

zoegirl: it's just . . . i really like talking to mr. h., that's all.

zoegirl: i'm not gonna start wearing huge crosses around my neck, and i'm not gonna replace madigan with cherryl ann booth. geez.

SnowAngel: i know. don't worry.

zoegirl: anyway, that's why i called—cuz of friday morning fellowship. i know it's dumb, but what should i wear?

Send	Cancel	

SnowAngel:	dumb? *widens eyes* zoe, fashion is NEVER dumb!
zoegirl:	soooo?
SnowAngel:	well, zoe dear, it's all about the details. say, for example, i'm getting ready for a date . . . hey, wait a minute! i AM getting ready for a date!
zoegirl:	go on
SnowAngel:	and say i put powder on my nose to get rid of the shininess, and i use just a dab of cheek tint to get that flushed-and-glowing look, and i curl my eyelashes for ten seconds on each side and put on one coat of black mascara, AFTER gently wiping the wand on a square of toilet paper to de-glumpify it . . . well, say i do all that, but i forget to pluck the nasty and annoying chin hair that appears like clockwork a week before i get my period. (not that i ever would forget. i HATE that chin hair.) but say i did, do u think rob would fall to his knees and worship me for the goddess i am?
zoegirl:	um . . .
SnowAngel:	i think not
zoegirl:	so what should i wear?
SnowAngel:	let's do a visual, shall we? *whips out artist's palette and jaunty beret* Portrait of Zoe on a Typical Day: shiny brown hair in cute little bob, big brown eyes, shy smile. so far, so good, which is lucky since u can't do much about your basic face. u COULD flip out the ends of your hair and add some wax for an edgier look, but blah, blah, blah, i know u won't.
zoegirl:	i look stupid when i try to do my hair some fancy way. we have gone over this before.

Send   Cancel

37

SnowAngel:	zoe, zoe, zoe. even mormon girls use wax, like carmen on american idol 2, remember?
zoegirl:	no
SnowAngel:	and she looked sweet AND hot. but whatever, let's move on. i know u like the baggie look, but sweetie, it's time to step into the new millenium.
zoegirl:	and again i ask: so what should i wear?
SnowAngel:	hmm, it's a school thing, not a date, even tho it's at some guy's house. u wanna be comfy and casual, but still look good. i say u can't go wrong with jeans and a white t-shirt. NOT your dad's vanderbilt shirt. one that fits. do u own one that fits?
zoegirl:	u don't think that's boring, jeans and a t-shirt?
SnowAngel:	think classic, zoe. not boring. wear your brown leather belt, your brown doc martens, a pair of funky earrings, and ur good to go.
zoegirl:	what about u? what r u wearing to the dark horse?
SnowAngel:	well since u asked. attire: pink spongebob "bubble bath" t-shirt, jeans, pink clogs, hair in a jillion clippies. scent: "leap," from the body shop. makeup: standard, but with thicker eyeliner on upper lids for that over-21 look. what do u think?
zoegirl:	lovely, dahling
SnowAngel:	*kisses all around* and now i simply must run. gotta go pluck that chin hair!

Thursday, September 16, 11:03 PM

SnowAngel:	i'm in heaven!!! simply heaven!!!
zoegirl:	hey, angela. i am SO sorry, but i was seriously just about to sign off. i am soooo tired.
SnowAngel:	don't u wanna hear about my romantic evening? i IMed u cuz i knew your mom would kill me if i called this late.
zoegirl:	i do wanna hear about it, and u can tell me all about it tomorrow. find me before homeroom, ok?
SnowAngel:	but, zoe! i think he may be THE ONE.
zoegirl:	the "one" what?
SnowAngel:	*lowers voice to stage whisper* the one i go all the way with (!!!)
zoegirl:	oh, god
SnowAngel:	i'm saying MAYBE, that's all. IF things keep going well—and i know they will. *swoons* making love with rob would be amazing, i just know it.
zoegirl:	and how, exactly, do u know it?
SnowAngel:	cuz at least i've done more than kiss a guy, that's how.
SnowAngel:	anyway, one of us has to go for it eventually so she can tell the others what it's like. and not to be rude, but it's not gonna be u or maddie.
zoegirl:	oh. well, now that i know ur really doing it for us . . .
SnowAngel:	haha, very funny
zoegirl:	i'm just glad ur not rushing into things, that's all i'm saying. i'm just glad u went out with him on 2 whole dates before making this decision.

Send   Cancel

SnowAngel: rob and i have a true connection, zoe. u know i'm never wrong about these things!

zoegirl: ohhhh, right. silly me. and now i have GOT to go to bed. good nite!!!

Friday, September 17, 5:15 PM

mad maddie: s'up, peepz? u heading over for our friday nite festivities?

zoegirl: i'll be there in 10 minutes. want me to bring anything?

mad maddie: yo dancin ass, baby, cuz dmx is crankin and i'm ready to groove. (er, if you won't be offended, that is. they do say the f-word, u know.)

zoegirl: will u please shut up? what about angela—is her mom gonna drop her off?

mad maddie: yes'm, and we can tease her about her loverboy some more. "oh, he is so amazing. every moment at the dark horse was something special. i really think he's the one!!!"

zoegirl: u don't really think she's gonna sleep with him, do u?

mad maddie: r u serious? she may be a fool, our angela, but she's no skank.

zoegirl: i never said she was!

mad maddie: anywayz, rob'll be long gone before things get that far. especially if angela's been feeding him the same hoo-ha she's been feeding us.

zoegirl: i guess

zoegirl: but it kinda freaks me out that she'd even consider the possibility.

mad maddie: what, u don't think about it? ever?

mad maddie: oh, wait, ur saint zoe. of course u don't.

40

zoegirl: screw u. i THINK about it, but that's all.

mad maddie: well, that's all angela's doing. it's just, u know, the next stage in her "this is true love and i am a fairy princess" fantasy. she thought about it with dixon schaeffer 2, remember? and that scott guy from the pool?

zoegirl: oh, yeah. she did, didn't she?

mad maddie: and now, enuff chit-chat. get yo-self over here!

zoegirl: ok. c ya soon!

Saturday, September 18, 4:00 PM

SnowAngel: omg, this sucks.

mad maddie: what sucks?

SnowAngel: me, my life, MY MOM. the fact that it's saturday nite and i'm stuck at home with chrissy, who's watching a "7th heaven" marathon on the WB. this SUPER sucks.

mad maddie: oh, that's right. zoe called and told me u'd been grounded, but she didn't give me the full story.

SnowAngel: i should have known something was wrong when mom picked me up from your house. she was all "hello, angela" in this frosty, ice-queen way, but i didn't care cuz rob and i were SUPPOSED to go to a movie tonite and i was imagining the romantic possibilities of snuggling in the theater together. but mom axed all of that, thank u very much.

mad maddie: cuz she found out u'd lied to her?

SnowAngel: aaargh! it is SO not a big deal, but she's making it out to be a federal case. she waited til we were halfway home and then she said, "angela, i

	read a note in your french book, and i know u didn't go to the library thursday nite."
mad maddie:	**ouch**
SnowAngel:	she was like, "how can i trust u? u continually deceive me. ur the only member of the family who is dishonest, angela, and i consider this a character flaw."
mad maddie:	**a character flaw—yikes. the moms hasn't laid that one on me yet.**
SnowAngel:	i just kinda plummeted inside myself, the way i always do when i'm confronted with something "wrong" that i've done. thank god she didn't realize it was a bar i'd gone to—then i'd really be dead. she just thinks i met up with rob and hung out, but apparently that's bad enuff, cuz now i'm stuck at home with my 12-year-old sister while matt tries to stop his ex's wedding.
mad maddie:	**ooo, the one where matt sees heather's fiance kissing someone else and he doesn't know if he should tell her? and he's got that lanky haircut but he's still a total hottie?**
SnowAngel:	das de one
mad maddie:	**i might have to get off soon. i LOVED that episode.**
SnowAngel:	bike over and watch it with us! please, please, please!!!
mad maddie:	**god, r we pathetic**
SnowAngel:	actually, i think there r a lot of closet fans of that show . . .
mad maddie:	**but anywayz, i can't. i've got to go to work.**

Send   Cancel

SnowAngel:	yeah, yeah. zoe's out with her parents, ur off to serve beignets with that cute waiter guy, and here i'll be, drowning myself in an endless pool of misery. 😞
mad maddie:	**it could be worse.**
SnowAngel:	how?
mad maddie:	**chrissy could be watching a "lizzie mcguire" marathon.**
SnowAngel:	oh god. this so sucks!!! i was like; "ok, mom, fine. i've learned my lesson. now can i please go out?" i totally begged her, and she still said no. i hate her! she is ruining my life!
mad maddie:	**damn her oily hide**
SnowAngel:	i'm serious!
mad maddie:	**i know, but i've g2g. i've gotta get dressed for work. r we still doing our math together tomorrow?**
SnowAngel:	yeah. i'm allowed to do homework with ppl, i just can't go out with rob. i feel so bad for him, cuz now HIS nite is totally ruined 2.
mad maddie:	**if u say so**
SnowAngel:	*sniffles pathetically* bye!

Saturday, September 18, 4:23 PM

mad maddie:	**me again**
SnowAngel:	r u coming over?!!
mad maddie:	**i'm WORKING, u freak. must we go over this again?**
mad maddie:	**i just wanted to ask—did u notice that zoe didn't mention friday morning fellowship at all last nite?**
SnowAngel:	well, duh. cuz she knew u'd make fun of her.
mad maddie:	**and get damned to hell? heavens, no.**

Send   Cancel

SnowAngel:	yes, ur so sensitive that way.
mad maddie:	**whatevs. is she going back next friday?**
SnowAngel:	*sigh* must we talk about this now? i'm really 2 depressed to deal with it.
mad maddie:	**just tell me**
SnowAngel:	she said the drive with mr. h was really good, and they had this great talk about relativism and what a cop-out it is, or something like that. so i think she's going back, yes.
mad maddie:	**blah**
SnowAngel:	blah yourself
mad maddie:	**well, byeas!**
SnowAngel:	sure, just leave me here to rot. don't think i don't care!!!

Monday, September 20, 4:45 PM

SnowAngel:	zooooeeeeeee! *stomp stomp stomp*
zoegirl:	angelaaaaaa! why the stomping?
SnowAngel:	cuz i'm pissed!!!!! 😩
zoegirl:	why?
SnowAngel:	CUZ! cuz stupid rob went out anyway, and he didn't even tell me!
zoegirl:	angela, what r u talking about?
SnowAngel:	i was heading out after school, and tonnie wyndham came twiddling over and said, "i hear ur going out with rob. that's great!" only she didn't say it like it was great. she said it in this fake-surprised way, like rob's dating down or something cuz i'm not a cheerleader.

44

zoegirl:	tonnie is a spaz
SnowAngel:	she's a superficial psycho-slut. i said, "yeah, we've only been dating for a week, but it seems like so much longer. we totally have this awesome connection." and tonnie was like, "i know. that's why it was so sad that u couldn't come with us saturday nite." and i was like, "huh?" and she goes, "me and rob and tim and eric. didn't rob tell u?"
zoegirl:	he went out with tonnie? while u were grounded?
SnowAngel:	well, they didn't GO OUT go out.
SnowAngel:	they just, u know, hung together at eric's house.
zoegirl:	still!
SnowAngel:	it gets worse. cuz then rob strolls up, and i was like, "sounds like u had a good time saturday nite. u could have called me, u know." and tonnie goes, "he wanted to, but i told him not to." i said, "oh yeah, sure," and rob said, "really, angie. i was punching in your number and everything, and tonnie said to bag it. she said it would just bum u out to know that we were having such a blast without u."
zoegirl:	!!! what did tonnie say?
SnowAngel:	she didn't say anything. she just stood there pretending to be all sympathetic, nodding away like one of those bobble-head dogs.
zoegirl:	so what did u say to rob?
SnowAngel:	i said, "hey, no problem," but the whole thing makes me so mad! i just can't stand it that rob was going to call me and tonnie told him not to. SHE IS NOT THE BOSS OF HIM!

Send   Cancel

zoegirl:	yuck, yuck, yuck. why didn't he just call anyway?
SnowAngel:	cuz he's nice. cuz he was trying to do the right thing, and he probably thought it would bum me out. which it would have, but it still would have been better than nothing.
SnowAngel:	ANYWAY, i told him to call me when he got home, so i better get off in case he's trying right now.
zoegirl:	ok. don't let tonnie get u down.
SnowAngel:	ur so right. bye!

Tuesday, September 21, 5:34 PM

mad maddie:	**zo-ster!**
zoegirl:	madster!
mad maddie:	**i just got home from some excellent driving practice and found a long ass message from angela on my voice mail. i tried calling back, but she's not answering her cell.**
zoegirl:	i think she went shopping with chrissy. maybe she forgot to bring it.
mad maddie:	**why does she even have a cell if she always forgets to bring it with her?**
mad maddie:	**is she still being a pouty-pants about rob?**
zoegirl:	pretty much. she saw him talking to tonnie in the hall today or something.
mad maddie:	**ooo—talking in the hall. tsk, tsk.**
zoegirl:	i know, she's kinda overreacting.
mad maddie:	**she's moved straight from her starry-eyed phase into her wounded lover stage. which is good, if for no other reason, than cuz she's at least cut back with the devirginization business.**

Send   Cancel

zoegirl:	there is that
mad maddie:	**did she tell u what happened in math?**
zoegirl:	does it have to do with devirginization?
mad maddie:	**no, it has to do with her being all mopey cuz she's NOT gonna be devirginized. and before i explain, u've got to understand that usually in math class angela IS THE BIGGEST CHATTERBOX EVER.**
zoegirl:	no!
mad maddie:	**yes! and usually mr. miklos has to get all over her to make her shut up. well today, mr. miklos was like, "what test do u want on friday, a 1, 2, or 3?"**
zoegirl:	huh?
mad maddie:	**ohhhhhh, right. ur in smart math, so u dunno about this. in dumb math whenever we have a test, it can either be a series 1, 2, or 3, with 3 being the hardest. not that even a 3 would be hard for u, of course, but for us dummies, it can be quite traumatic.**
zoegirl:	maddie . . .
mad maddie:	**so mr. miklos said, "should i choose, or should we have a game of chance?" we didn't want the devil choosing, so we took the game of chance. he put three marbles in a bag and said that if he pulled out a red marble, we'd have a 1, if he pulled out a blue one, we'd have a 2, and if he pulled out a white one, we'd have a 3. first he pulled out a blue one, and we were like, "no fair!" so he tried again and pulled out a white one, and everyone was like, "cheat! do-over, do-over!" so finally i said, "hey, mr. miklos, how about if angela doesn't say a word for the entire class. THEN will u give us a series 1?"**

Send   Cancel

zoegirl:	did he go for it?
mad maddie:	**HA! mr. miklos thought there was no way angela could do it, but angela sat there glum and depressed for the WHOLE CLASS! it was awesome!**
zoegirl:	what did angela think of all this?
mad maddie:	**i teased her about it afterward, and she got all grunty and spouted off. but i'm sorry—if she's going to be depressed, we might as well get something good out of it.**
zoegirl:	ha
zoegirl:	so how'd the driving go? all set for your license?
mad maddie:	**u know it. today i drove on northside parkway for the very first time.**
zoegirl:	was it scary?
mad maddie:	**it was a little freaky with all those cars behind me. i was like, "ahhh! pressure!" and the moms was like, "slow down! slow down!" and her foot kept pumping away at her own pretend brake on her side of the car. thank GOD they don't have those driver's ed cars for sale, the ones with the real brake on the passenger side. the moms would be in heaven.**
zoegirl:	how long did u go for?
mad maddie:	**i drove down northside and then turned on mount paran and headed home. i didn't feel like trying to park. i can't do that for crap.**
zoegirl:	me neither
mad maddie:	**yeah, right. so listen, i'm forwarding u and angela a quiz called "what pattern r u?" go take it and then come back and tell me what u r.**
zoegirl:	what pattern am i? what pattern r u?

mad maddie:	**i am LEOPARD PRINT, baby. rebellious, independent, and unique.**
zoegirl:	ok-k-k-a-a-ay
mad maddie:	**so go take it!**
zoegirl:	brb!

Tuesday, September 21, 5:58 PM

zoegirl:	oh, maddie . . .
mad maddie:	**yes?**
zoegirl:	i'm STRIPES. refined, classic, and modest.
mad maddie:	**stripes, eh? i can c that. when ur not wearing your dad's ratty old vanderbilt shirt, that is.**
zoegirl:	yeah, and i can c u as leopard print—when ur not wearing jeans and your shit-stomping boots, that is.
mad maddie:	**i love my shit-stomping boots. byeas!**

Wednesday, September 22, 9:02 PM

mad maddie:	**angela-spangela!**
SnowAngel:	madigan-smadigan!
mad maddie:	**u will not BELIEVE what just happened.**
SnowAngel:	does it have to do with rob and tonnie? cuz i just don't think i can take anymore. she's trying to steal him away from me. i KNOW she is.
mad maddie:	**god, angela, could u be more obsessed? no, it doesn't have to do with rob or tonnie. i has to do with jana. i ran into her when i was shuttling the moms around this afternoon.**
SnowAngel:	eee-gads. if it's not one psycho-slut it's the other. where'd u c her?

mad maddie: at 7-11. the moms had to go to kroger to get the pops more beer (now isn't THAT a good role model), so i was killing time before we drove back home.

mad maddie: i'm getting totally smooth at changing lanes, btw. i'm gonna nail my driver's test.

SnowAngel: so what about jana?

mad maddie: well, jana and terri were standing by the magazines when i came in. margie walker was there 2, altho she wasn't with jana and terri, of course.

SnowAngel: of course

mad maddie: so jana and terri start checking out margie's new do, and jana's all, "god, margie. u have got to stop screwing with your hair."

SnowAngel: typical. god, let margie be a sk8r grrl if that's what she wants to be. what skin is it off jana's nose?

mad maddie: actually, it was the tiniest bit funny. i mean, i'm surprised margie has any hair left, the way she's always dyeing it and cutting it and shit. anywayz, margie left with her coffee and a scowl, and i walked past jana and terri to get to the slurpee machine. i gave them a quick nod, but that's all.

SnowAngel: good for u. not everyone's gonna fawn all over her, which is a good thing for jana to know.

mad maddie: yeah, but then terri left, and it was just me and jana in the store. so jana puts down her cosmo and strolls to the slurpee machine. she goes, "hey, maddie. what's up?" and we, like, had an honest-to-god conversation. it was so weird.

SnowAngel: i'll say. so what'd u talk about?

Send   Cancel

mad maddie: stupid stuff, like how she wishes they'd bring sour cherry slurpees back and crap like that. and i was like, "i am so with u. enuff of this strawberry-kiwi garbage! bring back the real flavors!" then she asked if i'd driven to 7-11 myself, and i told her no, but that i'd be getting my license in like 2 weeks. and she was all, "i am soooo jealous. i hate having to depend on my mom for rides, and my bday's not til april." i guess all of her friends have late bdays 2, which sucks.

SnowAngel: so true. whereas we, on the other hand, will have the luverly mads to chauffeur us around.

mad maddie: u got that straight

SnowAngel: well, that's totally bizarre that jana lowered herself enuff to talk to u. she was really scraping the bottom of the barrel, huh?

SnowAngel: u know i'm kidding

mad maddie: i know. but don't worry, i'm sure she'll go back to ignoring me at school tomorrow.

SnowAngel: why would i worry? i don't give a damn what jana does.

mad maddie: right. me neither.

mad maddie: HEY, didja take the pattern quiz?

SnowAngel: u would have to ask, wouldn't u? YES, i took the pattern quiz, and u know what it said i am? TIE-DYE! *pulls hair by roots*

mad maddie: what's wrong with tie-dye?

SnowAngel: do i wear birkenstocks? noooooooo. do i smell nastily of patchouli? nooooooo. do i write all my english papers on the legalization of marijuana? noooooooo and noooooooo again!!!!!

Send Cancel

mad maddie:	u liked what the quiz had to say, then.
SnowAngel:	please. tie-dye is SOOOOOOO last decade.
mad maddie:	pelt-woman wears tie-dyes all the time.
SnowAngel:	pelt-woman?
mad maddie:	mark's girlfriend, remember?
SnowAngel:	ur comparing me to the chick who doesn't shave her pubes?
mad maddie:	yep. i'm leopard print, btw. did i tell u that? i think the quiz had a lot to offer, really.
SnowAngel:	well i think my bed has a lot to offer. good nite, mads.
mad maddie:	nite, angela. i'll bring u that hemp necklace tomorrow.
SnowAngel:	NOT funny!!!

Thursday, September 23, 9:01 PM

SnowAngel:	zoe, thank god ur on-line! *wails and gnashes teeth* rob asked tonnie wyndham to go to carl's party with me and him on friday!!!
zoegirl:	what?!
SnowAngel:	remember when u left, after talking to me and rob in the hall? well, right as i was getting my books together, tonnie flounced up and starts telling rob how he was soooooooooo funny during english and how it was sooooooooo great that he got mr. kirk to give everyone an extension on their papers. and i was like, "go away, tonnie! u r soooooooo annoying and that t-shirt is soooooooooo ugly!" it was super super tight and had the word "trouble" written across it in sequins. *gag*

Send   Cancel

zoegirl:	did u really say that to her, that she was annoying?
SnowAngel:	no, but i wanted to.
SnowAngel:	so tonnie says, "what r u 2 luvbirds up to this weekend?" and very sweetly i grabbed rob's hand and said, "nothing much, just hanging out." rob goes, "what about carl's party? aren't we going to carl's party?" and tonnie squeals, "carl balkin? r his parents going out of town?" and rob goes, "yeah. u should come. right, angela?"
zoegirl:	what did u say???
SnowAngel:	i said, "oh, i wish u could, but it's only for ppl who don't wear sequins. sorry!"
zoegirl:	REALLY?
SnowAngel:	no. so now tonnie's coming with us to carl's tomorrow nite. we're even picking her up! *throws self off cliff*
zoegirl:	yuck. is she honestly hitting on rob, or is she just clueless?
SnowAngel:	do u even have to ask? on the way home i said to rob, all jokey, "guess u've got a date with 2 girls now. ooo—menage a trois!" he laffed, but he shot me this look like he was kinda nervous.
SnowAngel:	ANYWAY, if tonnie's coming to carl's, then u and maddie have to come 2, cuz i'll need u for moral support. ok?
zoegirl:	angela . . .
SnowAngel:	what?
zoegirl:	i hate those kinds of parties. u know that. where everyone gets all stupid and i feel like a loser cuz i don't drink.

Send   Cancel

SnowAngel:	no one cares that u don't drink. u have to come. please? u can just hold a beer and take little sips every so often.
zoegirl:	i don't wanna take little sips every so often. i hate beer.
SnowAngel:	then i'll pour a sprite in a cup for u and we'll tell everyone it's a wine cooler. no one cares!!!
zoegirl:	i don't know. my mom would kill me.
zoegirl:	what did maddie say?
SnowAngel:	i haven't asked her yet, but i'm sure she'll come. please, please, please, please, please? u can spy on tonnie and rob for me!
zoegirl:	grrrrrrrr
SnowAngel:	PLEASE???
zoegirl:	fine, all right. but i'll have to come home with u from school so i can call mom from there and she can c your number on caller i.d. and maybe i just won't mention the party at all.
SnowAngel:	*SUPERFLYINGTACKLEPOUNCE!* yay! it's gonna be so much fun—we can make snide remarks to each other and roll our eyes whenever tonnie says anything!!!
zoegirl:	wh-hoo!
SnowAngel:	OH! and speaking of parties, we have GOT to plan maddie's surprise party. her bday's 2 weeks from tomorrow!
zoegirl:	god, ur right
SnowAngel:	i think we should have it at collier park. everybody can bring food and we'll have a twilight picnic.
zoegirl:	who should we invite besides megan and kristin and mary kate?

Send   Cancel

SnowAngel:	tonnie? *throws head back and laffs maniacally* jana whitaker? *collapses in a heap of amusement*
zoegirl:	having fun?
SnowAngel:	oh, i crack myself up.
zoegirl:	did u c jana in the cafeteria line, tho? maddie was standing behind her, and they were chatting away like it was perfectly normal.
SnowAngel:	yeah, that was creepy. later i was like, "maddie? is there something u want to tell me?" and she goes, "jana's not as bad as i thought she was. she's actually kinda funny."
zoegirl:	WEIRD
SnowAngel:	i know
SnowAngel:	but i was kidding when i said we should invite her. (obviously)
zoegirl:	what about delia hardwick? she's in homeroom with me and maddie, and she seems pretty cool.
SnowAngel:	sure. let's start telling ppl tomorrow.
zoegirl:	ok. only i might not c delia, cuz i'll probably be late to homeroom.
SnowAngel:	cuz of friday morning fellowship?
zoegirl:	yeah. last week we didn't get back until the beginning of 1st period.
SnowAngel:	what did ms. andrist say?
zoegirl:	she didn't care.
SnowAngel:	hmmph. she would if it were a coven meeting.
SnowAngel:	hey, did u hear that announcement about the shakespeare festival? "this year we will not accept

Send   Cancel

55

	any booths concerning witchcraft or fortune telling unless they specifically pertain to shakespeare's plays."
zoegirl:	that sucks, i guess. do u care?
SnowAngel:	no
zoegirl:	me neither
SnowAngel:	ok, i'm off. c u tomorrow!

Thursday, September 23, 11:15 PM

mad maddie:	**zoe-girl! it's after 11:00 and ur still up. u rebel!**
zoegirl:	i was just finishing some research for my english paper.
mad maddie:	**ooo, for mr. h? kissy, kissy.**
zoegirl:	shut up
mad maddie:	**ur not going to that fellowship thing again tomorrow, r u?**
zoegirl:	i am, and again, shut up.
zoegirl:	is this why u IMed me? to make fun of my religious convictions?
mad maddie:	**since when did u have religious convictions? anywayz, no. i wanted to make fun of angela, about this dumb party she's dragging us to.**
zoegirl:	she called u, huh?
mad maddie:	**she needs to lighten up about this whole rob and tonnie deal. if there IS something going on b/w rob and tonnie, then angela should drop rob on his ass and be done with it. and if there ISN'T, then rob should drop angela on hers, cuz i'm sure she's driving him just as nuts as she's driving us.**
zoegirl:	u don't think tonnie's t-r-o-u-b-l-e?

Send   Cancel

mad maddie:	**HA! she bitched about that to u 2! when u KNOW she would totally wear that shirt herself if she'd found it first.**
zoegirl:	that thought did kinda cross my mind.
mad maddie:	**ah, well. so we'll go to this party at carl's and it'll be stupid, but that's ok cuz we'll be together.**
zoegirl:	yeah, but don't say anything to my mom about it. (not that u would.) hey, i've gotta go to bed. i'm zonked.
mad maddie:	**me 2. i changed my very own sheets this afternoon, btw. i feel so virtuous.**
zoegirl:	impressive
mad maddie:	**it'd been like a month. they were starting to reek. tootles!**

Friday, September 24, 7:29 PM

SnowAngel:	maddie, get off the computer! ur supposed to be getting dolled up for the party!
mad maddie:	**angela, u promised u weren't gonna get all freaky about this.**
SnowAngel:	yeah, but zoe's here and rob's gonna be here any minute, and then we're coming to pick up u and stupid tonnie. ☺ i just want everything to go well.
mad maddie:	**lighten up—it's just a party.**
mad maddie:	**so what r u wearing? i know that's the real reason u IMed.**
SnowAngel:	well . . . i suppose i've got time to tell u. attire: swirly dragon t-shirt, flared blue jeans, sapphire ring, silver i.d. bracelet, doc martens. scent: vanilla musk.
mad maddie:	**fab**

Send   Cancel

SnowAngel:	and u?
mad maddie:	**gray sweats and the pops' wife-beater shirt**
SnowAngel:	maddie!
mad maddie:	**jk**
SnowAngel:	eeek—rob's here! he just pulled in the drive. C U SOON!!!

Saturday, September 25, 10:43 AM

mad maddie:	**hey, zoe**
zoegirl:	hey, mads. what's up?
mad maddie:	**nothing, just lounging around being lazy. some party last nite, eh?**
zoegirl:	ack. it totally made me remember why i hate parties.
mad maddie:	**i know what u mean. i always feel so awkward, like i don't belong.**
zoegirl:	yeah, right, miss thang. i saw u shaking your booty to that ABBA cd. u were, like, leading a whole line dance.
mad maddie:	**for your information, i was dancing ironically.**
zoegirl:	u were a dancing fool
mad maddie:	**whatevs. it's cuz i had a couple of beers, that's all.**
zoegirl:	uh . . . yeah. everybody had a couple of beers except for me, even kristin and megan who last year didn't drink at all. and then everyone looked at me like "ooo, geek girl," like i was gonna report them to the honor council or something.
mad maddie:	**so just have a beer, for crying out loud!**
zoegirl:	no, thanks.
mad maddie:	**is it cuz of christ our lord? cuz he drank the wine, zo.**

Send   Cancel

zoegirl:	i'm not gonna drink just cuz other ppl do, thank u very much. it's stupid. mr. h told me that he used to be a total hellion, that he'd drive around with his buddies and bash in trashcans and stuff, but then he realized he was just doing it to be cool, and so he stopped. he says it takes strength to be true to yourself.
mad maddie:	**mr. h claimed to be a hellion?**
zoegirl:	well, yeah
mad maddie:	**he used that very word, didn't he? "hellion." it's like he's trying to be all bad-ass to impress u.**
zoegirl:	he also told me how he used to have all these headbanger cds, but he dumped them when he realized he was a christian.
mad maddie:	**this just gets better and better. does he tell everyone this stuff, or just u?**
zoegirl:	he's NICE, maddie. he, like, listens to me. he cares what i have to say.
zoegirl:	and i might as well tell u, i think i'm gonna go to church with him tomorrow.
mad maddie:	**wtf?!!**
zoegirl:	well, ok, i AM going to church with him tomorrow.
mad maddie:	**WTF?!!!!!**
zoegirl:	he invited me on the way to fellowship on friday, and it sounds cool. there's nothing wrong with trying it out.
mad maddie:	**zoe, r angela and i gonna have to hire a deprogrammer to come rescue u from some cabin? r u gonna become mr. h's luv slave?**
zoegirl:	u r a freak. it's a CHURCH, maddie.

Send   Cancel

mad maddie:	**how r u gonna get there? oh, god, is he picking u up? is this like a DATE?**
zoegirl:	maddie . . .
mad maddie:	**what does your mom say about all this?**
zoegirl:	unlike u, my mom is a normal person and thinks it's fine. she thinks it's good that i'm broadening my horizons.
mad maddie:	**that's 1 way to put it**
mad maddie:	**so IS he picking u up? u avoided the question.**
zoegirl:	yes, maddie, he's picking me up. but it's NO. BIG. DEAL.
mad maddie:	**uh huh. i still think it's extremely fishy.**
zoegirl:	i knew u were gonna act like this. i totally knew it. i thought, stupidly, that i should include u in my life. but your attitude is really bugging me.
mad maddie:	**well, sorreee**
zoegirl:	anyway, i've g2g. i've got a ton of homework to get started on.
mad maddie:	**but . . . but . . . we didn't get to gossip about rob and angela!**
zoegirl:	drat. bye!
mad maddie:	**did i tell u i saw rob grab tonnie's ass on the way to the keg?**
zoegirl:	u DID?
mad maddie:	**well, not exactly, but he did laff at her stupid jokes all nite. i hate "dumb blond" jokes, and i'm not even blond.**
zoegirl:	yes u are
mad maddie:	**i'm dirty blond. that doesn't count.**
zoegirl:	good-bye, maddie.
mad maddie:	**fine. byeas!**

Send   Cancel

Sunday, September 26, 11:32 AM

mad maddie: **hellooooooooo, angela.**

SnowAngel: hellooooooooo, madigan.

mad maddie: **lovely morning, isn't it? the birds r singing, the sun is shining, the bald man from across the street has shut off his cursed lawn mower . . .**

SnowAngel: what makes u so chipper today?

mad maddie: **moi? nothing, other than the fact that i had a great time at work last nite. speaking of, what happened to u and rob? i thought u 2 were gonna come by.**

SnowAngel: i thought so 2, but all rob wanted to do was hang out in his basement and play pool. he said he was still hungover from carl's party.

mad maddie: **oh. that sounds fun, i guess.**

SnowAngel: it was boring.

SnowAngel: what happened at huey's?

mad maddie: **the kitchen guy, sam, found a roach under one of the counters, a really, really big one with long, waving antennaes.**

SnowAngel: ewwwwww!

mad maddie: **it gets better. r u ready?**

SnowAngel: no

mad maddie: **he microwaved it.**

SnowAngel: maddie!!! EWWWWW!!!! ☺

mad maddie: **and then phil, the manager, came back and saw what was going on, cuz all the kitchen guys were cheering and making a lot of noise. he fired sam on the spot.**

SnowAngel: wow

mad maddie:	**yep**
SnowAngel:	and this is why u had such a great time at work? a roach got murdered and the kitchen guy was fired?
mad maddie:	**nooooooo, just be patient. remember that cute waiter ur always going on about?**
SnowAngel:	*perks up* the kinda shy one with the adorable dimples?
mad maddie:	**well, his name's ian. he and i were standing over to the side while all this was going on, and we kept giving each other looks, like, "do u believe these freaks?" and once he leaned close to say something, and his arm brushed mine.**
SnowAngel:	ah-HA!
mad maddie:	**and after work he lent me this cool sonny boy williams cd with these awesome blues songs on it.**
SnowAngel:	omg!!! *dance, dance*
mad maddie:	**calm down. he knows i like music, that's all.**
SnowAngel:	yeah right, that's all.
mad maddie:	**but it was still pretty cool.**
mad maddie:	**in fact, i think i'm gonna get off the computer and go flop down on my bed. relive my moment of passion and all that.**
SnowAngel:	buh-bye! way to go!!!!! *smiles all around for the fabulous mads!*

Monday, September 27, 7:19 PM

SnowAngel:	hey there, zoe
zoegirl:	hey, angela. what's up?
SnowAngel:	i didn't c u after 6th period and i have to know: was it

62

	weird seeing mr. h in class, after going to church with him and everything?
zoegirl:	it kinda was, actually. not bad-weird, just . . . weird, cuz i feel like i know him as so much more than a teacher, u know?
SnowAngel:	like how?
zoegirl:	we just had such good conversations on the way to and from alpharetta, where his church is. it was a long drive, so we got to talk A LOT. he's so interesting, angela, and he knows so much about spirituality. i know maddie makes fun of him, but i really admire him.
SnowAngel:	well, that's awesome. do u think HE thought it was weird today?
zoegirl:	i don't know. i may have been making it up. in fact, i probably was. but sometimes it seemed like he was giving me these looks, like he and i shared a secret. or not a secret, more like just the knowledge of the special time we had together.
zoegirl:	god, that sounds corny.
SnowAngel:	no, i know what u mean. that's cool.
zoegirl:	yeah, it really is.
SnowAngel:	don't get offended . . . but do u think he's hitting on u? just a little?
zoegirl:	PLEASE
zoegirl:	anyway, he told me that he doesn't believe in dating just for the sake of dating. he only wants to date someone if he thinks she might be a person he'd like to marry.
SnowAngel:	whoa. and ur not that person?
zoegirl:	i'm 15, angela.

Send   Cancel

SnowAngel:	so?
zoegirl:	altho something happened that was sort of funny. when he dropped me off after church, he reached over to open my door for me, and it was a little awkward cuz his body was, like, right there, u know? soooo close. and then he half-laffed and started to say something, but he stopped himself. i said, "what?" and he said, "i'll tell u when ur older."
SnowAngel:	zoe!!!!!
zoegirl:	DON'T tell maddie.
SnowAngel:	i won't ☹
SnowAngel:	but do u like him? as in, like him like him?
zoegirl:	he's my teacher, angela.
SnowAngel:	how old do u think he is, anyway?
zoegirl:	he's 24. he told me.
SnowAngel:	that's not that much older, zoe. that's only 9 years. my dad is 11 years older than my mom. *waggles eyebrows*
zoegirl:	well, it doesn't matter cuz he's my teacher. time to change the subject.
SnowAngel:	wow. u and mr. h.
zoegirl:	angela!
SnowAngel:	ok, ok. so u wanna hear something sad? chrissy got home from school today and said, "my friend lena thinks ur cute, but not pretty."
SnowAngel:	nice, huh?
zoegirl:	oh, angela. what does lena know, whoever she is?
SnowAngel:	i know, but it still bummed me out.

Send   Cancel

SnowAngel:	and then chrissy saw that she'd hurt my feelings, and she tried to apologize by telling me she loved me. the whole thing was pathetic.
zoegirl:	truly, angela. this lena chick is in 7th grade. she knows NOTHING.
SnowAngel:	aargh. u know what the worst part was? how ashamed i felt, in this embarrassed, low-down way.
zoegirl:	u have nothing to feel ashamed of, angela. first of all, u r TOTALLY pretty—u know ur the prettiest of u, me, and maddie—and second of all, chrissy adores u. it doesn't matter what anybody says.
SnowAngel:	but do u think chrissy's prettier than i am?
SnowAngel:	oh god, i can't believe i'm even asking this. *sticks head in toilet bowl out of pathetic-ness*
zoegirl:	chrissy's a kid, angela. she's got purple braces.
SnowAngel:	my mom thinks she's prettier. i know cuz one time i said it out loud, like, "i know chrissy's prettier than me, but that's ok," and mom didn't contradict me. she said we all have our special qualities.
zoegirl:	angela . . .
SnowAngel:	and to top everything off, rob is being a total penis-head. the only time i got to c him was before french, and he talked to matthew curtis the whole time, which pissed me off. but then i started thinking that it was just as much my fault that we didn't talk, so i called to c if i could go over and hang out, thinking maybe that would make everything fun again.
zoegirl:	and what did he say?
SnowAngel:	he had some friends over, so he said he'd call me back.

zoegirl:	and did he?
SnowAngel:	actually, yeah. he called me back and we talked for a while, and i thought i was being interesting, even tho he wasn't really responding. but then i finished telling him about a dream i'd had and there was absolute silence.
zoegirl:	oh, no
SnowAngel:	then really abruptly he goes, "well, i'll c u tomorrow, ok?" just out of the blue. it was seriously pretty rude.
zoegirl:	god, tell me about it.
SnowAngel:	he didn't say, "listen, angela, i've gotta go," or anything like that, he just went, "i'll c u tomorrow" smack in the middle of the conversation.
zoegirl:	he's an asshole
SnowAngel:	except he's NOT, zoe!
SnowAngel:	maybe it's not healthy to like someone as much as i like him, but i can't help it. when things are good b/w us, they're so so good. he's, like, my soulmate, i swear to god.
zoegirl:	i hate to point this out, but u've only been going out with him for a week and a half.
SnowAngel:	2 weeks exactly. today is our anniversary.
zoegirl:	angela . . .
SnowAngel:	i know, i know. but i think i've secretly been liking him for a lot longer, and that makes it so much more real.
zoegirl:	but r u sure he's worth it?
SnowAngel:	yes, i'm sure! i'm totally sure! except when he's being an asshole. *grinds teeth*

Send   Cancel

SnowAngel:	fine. ur right. i'm not gonna bother with him anymore until he shows a sign of wanting to be bothered.
zoegirl:	good. and anyway, we have maddie's bday party to focus on. i talked to delia in homeroom today—which was kinda tricky cuz i couldn't let maddie hear—and she's totally up for it. she's gonna bring chips and guac.
SnowAngel:	so everyone's coming except mary kate. i wish it was this weekend instead of next.
zoegirl:	i know. just don't let that other stuff get u down, ok?
SnowAngel:	i'll try
zoegirl:	i'm gonna stay on-line to do some research, so IM me again if u need to.
SnowAngel:	ok
zoegirl:	or call me. i won't be on for long.
SnowAngel:	thanks, zo
SnowAngel:	really, i'm fine—it's just been a crappy day. bye!

Tuesday, September 28, 10:15 PM

mad maddie:	**hey there, angela**
SnowAngel:	hey, maddie
mad maddie:	**did u have a better day today, even tho mr. miklos picked on u in math?**
SnowAngel:	i guess
SnowAngel:	things improved with rob, anyway.
mad maddie:	**meaning?**
SnowAngel:	meaning he apologized for getting off the phone with me so quickly yesterday.
mad maddie:	**that's good**

67

SnowAngel:	yeah. i acted all puzzled, like i didn't even know what he was talking about. then u know what i told him?
mad maddie:	**what?**
SnowAngel:	that i'd gone out and walked on the train tracks until midnite, just by myself.
mad maddie:	**u went to the train tracks? by yourself?**
SnowAngel:	hell no! r u crazy?
mad maddie:	**i was gonna say**
mad maddie:	**shit, ur always going on about how freaky they r, how ur afraid a hobo is gonna come and molest u.**
SnowAngel:	cuz one could, u never know.
mad maddie:	**so why'd u say that then? to rob?**
SnowAngel:	cuz i liked the idea of it. cuz i liked the idea of him thinking that i went out and walked all nite on the train tracks. it's a lot better than what i really did, which was lie on my bed and listen to jewel. *do you want me like i want you? or am i standing still beneath a darkened sky . . . was that you passing me by?*
mad maddie:	**u r lucky i am nice and will as a favor to you forget that you just said that and not tell anyone about it.**
SnowAngel:	*sticks out tongue*
SnowAngel:	but u know what's strange?
mad maddie:	**what?**
SnowAngel:	it made me start wondering how much of other ppl r just images they made up. like maybe ppl lie about all kinds of things—how would we ever know?
mad maddie:	**totally. like today in math, when carl balkin was sitting in the back guffawing with his buds about all the action**

Send   Cancel

	he got with some freshman chick. i was like, "yeah, right, carl. not even a freshman would get it on with u."
SnowAngel:	so true
mad maddie:	and that necklace he was wearing, with all the little metal balls? tray fruitay.
SnowAngel:	god, i know
SnowAngel:	but u shouldn't use that expression.
mad maddie:	what expression?
SnowAngel:	"tray fruitay." it's not nice.
mad maddie:	wtf? jana said it this morning in homeroom, and it cracked me up.
SnowAngel:	yeah, but it's like making fun of someone for being gay.
mad maddie:	no it's not, cuz it's an insult u could only use on someone who's not gay. if someone was trying to look gay on purpose then it would be no big deal. but if someone looks like an idiot just cuz he is an idiot, then it's his fault and he should be mocked.
SnowAngel:	but ur mocking him by calling him gay, which is mean to ppl who r gay.
mad maddie:	oh, please
SnowAngel:	u know i'm right
mad maddie:	but don't u think it's the slightest bit funny? tray fruitay?
SnowAngel:	i think it's funny that U think it's funny, given the fact that it comes from jana.
mad maddie:	ohhhhhhh. so it's wrong to use "gay" as an insult, but u can dismiss something just cuz a certain person said it and that's fine and dandy?
SnowAngel:	excuse me?

mad maddie:	**i just think ur being hypocritical, that's all.**
SnowAngel:	*steps a safe distance away* o-k-a-a-a-y . . .
mad maddie:	**just drop it. this is retarded.**
SnowAngel:	fine
mad maddie:	**fine**
SnowAngel:	i've g2g, anyway
mad maddie:	**whatevs**

Tuesday, September 28, 10:44 PM

mad maddie:	**zoe!**
zoegirl:	hey, maddie. what's up?
mad maddie:	**not much. i was IMing with angela and she pissed me off, that's all.**
zoegirl:	why r u pissed at angela? what'd she do?
mad maddie:	**nothing, it's stupid. anywayz, i was GOING to give her the personality quiz of the week, but i didn't, so i'm gonna give it to u instead.**
zoegirl:	lay it on me
mad maddie:	**it's called "Discover Ur Inner Dragon." wanna hear what it said about me?**
zoegirl:	sure
mad maddie:	***As the mighty Blades of old, your Dragon color is...COPPER. Coppers show up when someone's about to die. You like to stomp your enemies, incite rebellions, start the occasional war, and spend lazy hours preening your battle aura. Just in case some puny human thinks they can get the drop on you, you've got a concealed breath weapon—gigantic masses of Fire. Hey, it's the tried and true way to cook a cow in 0.75 seconds.***

zoegirl:	what the . . . ? that is weird, maddie. i don't even know what it's talking about.
mad maddie:	**it's talking about how tough i am, that's what.**
zoegirl:	i suppose. where do u find these things?
mad maddie:	**it's one of my many talents. so r u ready to discover your own inner dragon?**
zoegirl:	if i must
mad maddie:	**go to geocities.com and type in "dragon"—that'll get u to the quiz. then report back to me.**
zoegirl:	yes, ma'am
mad maddie:	**cyas!**

Tuesday, September 28, 10:59 PM

zoegirl:	hey, mads. i'm back.
mad maddie:	**and?**
zoegirl:	*As the Day that cleanses and gives Life, your Dragon color is...WHITE. You reach for spirituality and look down upon the world from the highest mountain peaks. If someone ever threatens you, your Inner Dragon would likely tell you to hit and run, or just plain run. But if they really wanted a fight you'd be an impressive opponent, considering you pack a breath weapon combination of Fire and Lightning. Even the nicest dragons can do some serious damage.*
mad maddie:	**c?! it's u to a T, especially the bit about reaching for spirituality. (if that's what u call flirting with mr. h, anywayz)**
zoegirl:	ha ha, very funny

mad maddie:	**c'mon, how can u not luv these things? i'm gonna email the site to angela after all, cuz i have to know what she is. betcha a million her color's pink.**
zoegirl:	do dragons come in pink?
mad maddie:	**hell, i didn't know they came in white. ttfn!**

Wednesday, September 29, 7:02 PM

mad maddie:	**three warm chocolate chip cookies, courtesy of the pillsbury dough boy. IN. MY. BELLY.**
SnowAngel:	mmmm. I☺I and hello to u 2, miss maddie.
mad maddie:	**so guess what? ONLY 1 WEEK AND 2 DAYS TIL MY BIRTHDAY!!!**
SnowAngel:	wh-hoo! *wild, arm-flailing cheerleader jumps*
mad maddie:	**i can't freakin wait. the moms promised to take me to get my license that very afternoon, as soon as school lets out.**
SnowAngel:	r u scared?
mad maddie:	**not about the written part, but i'm jittery about the actual driving part. i know i can do all the stuff, but what if i spaz out with the testing guy there in the car with me?**
SnowAngel:	i know. my bday's not for three more months, but i still get sweaty thinking about it. ESPECIALLY parallel parking.
mad maddie:	**did i tell u what happened when my brother took his test?**
SnowAngel:	no
mad maddie:	**he had to weave the car through these orange cones, and he ran over one with his back tire. the guy who was grading him shook his head and said, "sorry, son. u knock over a cone, ur done."**

Send   Cancel

SnowAngel:	oh no! that's TOTALLY gonna happen to me, i know it!
mad maddie:	**but when mark pulled forward, the cone sprang back up. the guy looked at the cone, looked at mark, and said, "all right. keep going."**
SnowAngel:	no way! HA!
SnowAngel:	did he end up passing the test?
mad maddie:	**barely**
SnowAngel:	that's hilarious
mad maddie:	**so i figure that even if i'm nervous, if mark could pass it then surely i can 2.**
SnowAngel:	r your parents gonna let u start driving right away? on your own, i mean?
mad maddie:	**well, i'll have my license, so they'll have to—it's the law. but yeah, they're ok with it cuz then i can be their slave girl and do errands for them and shit. the pops had the gremlin checked over by his mechanic, and everything's looking good.**
SnowAngel:	IT IS GONNA BE SO AWESOME!!!! the winsome threesome, styling along in the gremlin. *queenly wave to crowds of fawning admirers*
mad maddie:	**u know what i've been thinking?**
SnowAngel:	what?
mad maddie:	**well, remember my road trip fantasy? i think we should go for it. like maybe after thanksgiving, over that long weekend. wouldn't that rock?**
SnowAngel:	for real? YES!!! YES, YES, YES, YES, YES!!!!
mad maddie:	**i know our parents r gonna shoot it down, especially zoe's. but if we start working on them now, maybe we can convince them.**

Send   Cancel

73

SnowAngel:	omg. we'll have to really plan it out so they can see how mature and responsible we're being.
mad maddie:	**yeah, so start thinking of places we could drive to, places that would be fun but that wouldn't push the rents over the edge. like maybe busch gardens?**
SnowAngel:	ooo—my cousin went there and said it's a blast. and seaworld is near there 2, right?
mad maddie:	**i think so. this whole idea may totally not happen—it probably won't—but it's worth a try.**
SnowAngel:	or maybe it will, cuz we'll MAKE it happen. oh, that would just be so cool. and it'll give us something to look forward to so we can last til thanksgiving.
mad maddie:	**i'll have had my license for 2 months by then, which hopefully will count for something.**
SnowAngel:	have u told zoe?
mad maddie:	**no, but i will. i'll call her after "that 70s show."**
SnowAngel:	haha. TOLD u u'd get hooked!
mad maddie:	**whatevs. quick, before i go: did u take the "become one with your inner dragon" quiz?**
SnowAngel:	oh, that. *rolls eyes*
mad maddie:	**and?**
SnowAngel:	and my results were completely dumb, only ur gonna think they're hysterical.
mad maddie:	**tell me. come on, come on, come on.**
SnowAngel:	*sighs loudly* As the vast forests that protect our planet, your dragon color is...GREEN. You like to commune with nature and lobby governments for alternative fuels and conservation. Folks shouldn't get the idea you're a hippy pushover though, because

Send   Cancel

	your breath weapon is a nasty fire/acid combination.
	Maybe you should invest in a hemp shirt reading
	"Don't knock my smock, or I'll clean your clock."
mad maddie:	**YES! first tie-dye and now communing with nature! u R a hippy chick!**
SnowAngel:	enuff
mad maddie:	**u and pelt-woman, baby. u should go have a moon ceremony together.**
SnowAngel:	excuse me, but do u want me to flame u with my breath weapon?
mad maddie:	**hee hee hee. i can just c u in a hemp shirt . . .**
SnowAngel:	*prepares to spit fire*
mad maddie:	**time for "that 70s show." l8rs, cheese gr8rs!**

Wednesday, September 29, 8:12 P.M.

mad maddie:	**is there any way we can get together and round out the back of hyde's head? it is totally bugging me.**
SnowAngel:	don't be mean. i think he's adorable.
mad maddie:	**and i'm sorry, but is donna a transvestite? her voice is SO deep. and her shoulders r broader than my dad's, i'm not kidding.**
SnowAngel:	it's back on. g2g!

Friday, October 1, 6:30 PM

SnowAngel:	zoe! *bangs on keys* what is WRONG with the world?!!!
zoegirl:	hmm. i'm guessing maybe u'll tell me?
SnowAngel:	what's wrong is that it's 6:30 on friday nite, which means i SHOULD be preparing for a romantic evening

	with my boyfriend. but am i? noooooooooo. he was supposed to call right after school to let me know what the plans were, and now it's three hours l8r and HE HASN'T FREAKIN CALLED!!!
zoegirl:	ack. have u called him?
SnowAngel:	i've left FIVE MESSAGES. no one's there.
zoegirl:	maybe he just forgot
SnowAngel:	if he did, that's even worse. *glares murderously*
SnowAngel:	do u know what happened today? do u? i found rob before lunch and he was standing by his locker talking to tonnie. he was asking for her advice on the sweater he was wearing, whether he should zip it or leave it unzipped. can u believe that?!!
zoegirl:	um . . . i'm not sure. i mean, i know it was bad for him to be talking to tonnie, but why do u care about the sweater? did u give it to him or something?
SnowAngel:	NO, i didn't give it to him. i just . . . aargh. the first time we went out he was wearing his moab shirt on top of a long-sleeve shirt, and he asked if i thought it was 2 much. 2 sk8rboy. at the time i thought it was sweet, the fact that he cared what he looked like. AND the fact that he wanted my opinion. then today i saw him playing the same game with tonnie and it just made me feel sick.
zoegirl:	yuck, angela. why don't u just break up with him?
SnowAngel:	i should, i totally should.
zoegirl:	so why don't u?
SnowAngel:	i dunno. *sighs* it's complicated.
zoegirl:	???

Send   Cancel

SnowAngel:	this'll sound weird, but it's like i can't just walk away from him cuz then i'd be this big loser. i mean, he's so amazingly smart and funny and adorable, so when i'm around him, i try really hard to be smart and funny and adorable, 2. it's like i have to earn his respect, u know?
SnowAngel:	i just . . . i wanna mean more to him than i do.
zoegirl:	oh, angela
SnowAngel:	i know
zoegirl:	ur not gonna wait around for him to call u, r u? please don't wait around for him to call.
SnowAngel:	don't worry. mom's taking me and chrissy to bennigan's cuz dad has a late meeting. MAYBE i'll try him again afterward, if i'm feeling nice.
zoegirl:	that's the spirit. (altho i c no reason to call him again. he should be calling u.)
SnowAngel:	ur right, ur right, ur right. let's talk about something else, ok? something cheerful.
zoegirl:	sure. what do u wanna talk about?
SnowAngel:	our road trip!!! *pumps fist in air and whoops like a redneck*
zoegirl:	oh, man. my mom is never gonna go for it.
SnowAngel:	but did madigan tell u her new idea, about cumberland island? it's way closer than busch gardens, and once we got there we could take a ferry to the island itself and camp out. it would just be us and the park rangers, so our parents wouldn't have to worry about us partying or anything.

ttyl	

zoegirl:	yeah, we talked about it in homeroom. jana whitaker was kinda listening in, and she said beach camping is really fun.
SnowAngel:	jana said that?
zoegirl:	uh huh. the whole time we were talking, jana was like, "road trip. yeah. that's cool." maddie acted as smooth as ever, but i could tell she was pleased.
SnowAngel:	GOD, that makes me sick.
zoegirl:	why?
SnowAngel:	cuz it's soooo not maddie—or at least it used to not be. these days i'm not so sure.
zoegirl:	what do u mean?
SnowAngel:	well, i don't even wanna get into it, cuz it's like the more we talk about jana the more power she gets. but today in math maddie was chatting up eric craver, and i heard her say that once she got her license, she was gonna "cruise the back roads and blast some totally cream music."
zoegirl:	blast some totally cream music?
SnowAngel:	it's her new jana-ism. it's just so disgusting how she's gone from hating her to, like, worshipping her.
zoegirl:	well, "worshipping" may be a little extreme. anyway, maybe jana's changed. maybe she's gotten better.
SnowAngel:	i can't believe u would even say that!!! do u know what jana said to me today? DO u? i was doing my nails during my free, and jana breezes up and goes, "saw u at carl's party with rob. d'ya getcha some?"
zoegirl:	getcha some what?
SnowAngel:	what do u think?!

Send	Cancel

SnowAngel:	and then she goes, "or was it tonnie who got lucky?" then she fake-laffed and was like, "just kidding. honestly, i think it's so big of u not to care that he flirts with other girls."
zoegirl:	oh, that's bad
SnowAngel:	do u think she knows something that i don't? do u really think he's flirting with tonnie?
zoegirl:	i don't think so. but i wouldn't worry about anything jana says.
zoegirl:	why didn't u tell us this at lunch?
SnowAngel:	cuz it made me totally paranoid, but what if maddie thought it was funny? cuz, u know, according to maddie, jana can do no wrong. anyway, the point is that jana is NOT a nice person.
zoegirl:	i guess not
zoegirl:	hey, listen. i'm heading off to an early movie with my parents. wanna come?
SnowAngel:	is it one of those artsy-fartsy subtitled ones they always drag u to?
zoegirl:	er . . .
SnowAngel:	no thanks. anyway, i'm going out with mom and chrissy, remember?
zoegirl:	oh yeah. well, try to have fun, and DON'T obsess about rob. he's not worth it.
SnowAngel:	ur so right. bye!

Friday, October 1, 9:45 PM

zoegirl:	maddie! get off the computer and get your butt over to angela's—NOW!

Send　　Cancel

mad maddie:	**???**
zoegirl:	she's been crying to me over the phone ever since i got home from my movie. we tried calling u 3-way, but your stupid line is busy.
mad maddie:	**probably mark talking to erin**
mad maddie:	**is everything ok? what happened?!**
zoegirl:	she ran into rob—WITH TONNIE. as in, on a date. angela went to bennigan's with her mom, and there they were: rob and tonnie, snuggled up over an awesome blossom.
mad maddie:	**christ, that sucks.**
mad maddie:	**what the hell is an awesome blossom?**
zoegirl:	u know, those fried onion thingies with the dipping sauce. angela and rob shared one on their first date 2.
mad maddie:	**that's right, angela and rob went to bennigan's 2! bet THAT went over really well.**
zoegirl:	seriously. angela is devastated, so i told her we'd come over and spend the nite. rent bad movies and pig out, that sort of thing.
mad maddie:	**sure, sounds good. i'll c if mark can give me a ride.**
zoegirl:	angela's all, "is it cuz tonnie's prettier than me? IS it?" i feel so bad for her.
mad maddie:	**did she say anything to rob when she saw him? did he c her?**
zoegirl:	he saw her, all right. angela said he stared at her for like 10 seconds, and then he turned to tonnie and started talking really animatedly, even tho a blush had spread from his neck all the way up his face. angela grabbed chrissy and her mom and jerked them out the door, and then she burst into tears.

Send   Cancel

mad maddie:	**that asshole**
zoegirl:	and then apparently her mom made some super supportive comment like, "just let it go, babe. he's obviously the type of boy who only cares about appearances." which i'm sure was SUPPOSED to make angela feel better, but totally didn't.
mad maddie:	**uh, yeah**
zoegirl:	so we should get over there, cuz she's totally a mess.
mad maddie:	**gotcha. cyas!**

Saturday, October 2, 5:22 PM

mad maddie:	**hey, poor sad angela. how ya doing?**
SnowAngel:	ever since u guys left this morning, i've done nothing but stuff my face with cool ranch doritos. i hate myself.
mad maddie:	**don't hate yourself, hate rob. have u talked to him yet?**
SnowAngel:	no
mad maddie:	**well, good. he's not worth it.**
SnowAngel:	i TELL myself that, but that's not how it feels.
SnowAngel:	i need u and zoe. ur the only ones who understand. u R coming back tonite, right?
mad maddie:	**ouch. that's actually why i IMed. i want to, but i can't. i can't find anyone to trade shifts with.**
SnowAngel:	no! u HAVE to!
mad maddie:	**but zoe'll be there. and i'll call u tomorrow, ok?**
mad maddie:	**i've g2g, cuz i'm supposed to be at huey's in 5 minutes. byeas!**

Send   Cancel

ttyl

Monday, October 4, 5:22 PM

SnowAngel: hey, mads. i had a totally crappy time at school today, just so u know. *sniffle, sniffle*

mad maddie: ah, shit. i'm sorry.

SnowAngel: i didn't wanna go at all, but mom made me. how unfair is that?

mad maddie: hey look, zoe's on-line.

Monday, October 4, 5:25 PM

SnowAngel: yeah, she just sent me an IM. she wants to know how i'm doing.

zoegirl: hey, angela. how's my girl?

mad maddie: well, don't tell her anything unless u tell me first .

SnowAngel: crappy. but thanks for asking.

SnowAngel: i won't, don't worry

zoegirl: aw, angela

mad maddie: i mean it

SnowAngel: hold on, i'm gonna set up a chat room so we can all talk.

SnowAngel: hey, i'm sending u a chat room invite, ok? just click on it so u and me and maddie can all talk together.

mad maddie: right on

zoegirl: ok, here goes . . .

You have just entered the room "Angela's Boudoir."
madmaddie has entered the room.
zoegirl has entered the room.

SnowAngel: check it out, eh? now we can all be miserable together.

mad maddie: sure nuff

Send   Cancel

zoegirl:	hey again, angela. and hey, mads!
mad maddie:	**so, angela, how was french? did u and rob talk, or did u blast him with your fiery breath weapon?**
zoegirl:	u have a fiery breath weapon 2? same here, only mine has lightning in it.
SnowAngel:	yes, rob and i talked. he said that tonnie was the one who asked him out, and he didn't know how to say "no."
mad maddie:	**that is the lamest excuse i think i've ever heard. please tell me u told him to go to hell.**
SnowAngel:	well, kinda. i told him it really hurt my feelings.
zoegirl:	good for u
mad maddie:	**what?!!! he treated u like dirt, angela. telling him he "really hurt your feelings" isn't gonna do it.**
SnowAngel:	that wasn't ALL he said. he also said that tonnie is just a friend, even if she wants to be more, and that he's sorry he ruined something good just cuz of her.
mad maddie:	**he's a dick. and he looks like david spade.**
SnowAngel:	he does not!
mad maddie:	**zoe?**
zoegirl:	well, not EXACTLY. but kinda.
mad maddie:	**c'mon. his forehead? his lips? his hair?**
SnowAngel:	i know. maybe i'll email him. cuz he acted like things were over b/w us when he was telling me about tonnie, but maybe that's just cuz he's afraid i won't give him a second chance.
mad maddie:	**ANGELA. STOP RIGHT NOW.**
SnowAngel:	but if it's true luv? i can't walk away from true luv!
zoegirl:	u REALLY think it's true love?

Send   Cancel

83

SnowAngel:	well, it MIGHT be. and i don't wanna be the kind of person who's not willing to put in the work, u know? love takes work. it's not all cake and ice cream.
mad maddie:	**all right, i can't deal with this. i'm outta here.**

mad maddie has left the room.

SnowAngel:	zoe? u still there?
zoegirl:	i'm still here
SnowAngel:	maddie doesn't get it, cuz she's never been in love. but it's better to have lived and loved than never to have lived at all.
zoegirl:	i guess
SnowAngel:	it's TRUE. and now i'm gonna email rob like i said i would, cuz u've made me feel so much better.
zoegirl:	i have?
SnowAngel:	thanks for the pep talk! bye!

Monday, October 4, 5:59 PM

zoegirl:	hey, mads. i just got off with angela. she's emailing rob right now.
mad maddie:	**oh, god. she is her own worst enemy, zoe. i am so serious.**
zoegirl:	i love her so much, but i do get kinda embarrassed for her, u know? but i don't know how to tell her that to her face.
mad maddie:	**tell me about it. i just wanna shake her shoulders and say, "GET A CLUE! HE IS A LOSER!!!"**
zoegirl:	i know. it's so sad.
mad maddie:	**yeah, but it's also just ANNOYING.**
mad maddie:	**hey, i didn't wanna mention it in front of angela, but can**

	i just tell u what a great time i had at work saturday nite?
zoegirl:	with ian?
mad maddie:	**we splashed dish water at each other—it was very flirty and fun. and get this: he asked if i wanted to hang out with him next weekend, after our shifts r over.**
zoegirl:	no way!
mad maddie:	**way!**
zoegirl:	u said yes, i'm assuming.
mad maddie:	**oh, i was very coy as i turned bright red and mumbled, "uh, sure!" i was quite the vixen.**
zoegirl:	man, u r gonna have an awesome bday weekend. u r still going out with me and angela on friday, right?
mad maddie:	**ack—i totally forgot. actually, the rents have had a rare moment of parental affection and wanna take me to that brazilian restaurant where u get heaps and heaps of meat. sounds like my kind of place, baby.**
zoegirl:	this friday? they're taking u out this friday?
mad maddie:	**uh, yes, since that would be my bday . . .**
zoegirl:	but u said u'd go out with us!
mad maddie:	**so we'll go out saturday instead, only it'll have to be in the morning since i work that nite. ooo—we could do the all-u-can-eat breakfast buffet at shoney's!**
zoegirl:	yeah, but angela had her heart set on being with u on your exact bday. i don't mean to make a big deal out of this, but she'll be really disappointed if we don't get together.
mad maddie:	**that's ridiculous**
zoegirl:	i know, but still. she'd be really, really disappointed.

Send   Cancel

ttyl

mad maddie:	**r u for real?**
zoegirl:	she's just so fragile right now.
mad maddie:	**fine. i'll tell the rents to take me out on saturday.**
zoegirl:	yes, that's a good idea. maybe THEY can take u to shoney's.
mad maddie:	**whatevs**
mad maddie:	**welp, time to bounce. mark is gonna take me driving in a minute here, and i must do my limbering up exercises. rotate the wrists, rotate the neck, practice my patented scan for dogs and small children . . .**
zoegirl:	have fun!
mad maddie:	**only four more days!!! adios!**

Monday, October 4, 7:45 PM

SnowAngel:	hi, zo. i wrote rob that email. i'm not gonna show it to maddie cuz she'd just be mean, but do u wanna read it?
zoegirl:	angela. r u sure rob's really worth it?
SnowAngel:	here's what it says: Dear Rob, I just wanted to say that it's totally cool if you want to hang out with other people. Obviously Tonnie is just a friend, because why would anyone choose her when they could have me? Ha ha, just joking. But anyway, we shouldn't let her come between us, because I think we have something really special. Call me, ok? Love, Angela.
zoegirl:	oh. well, that's . . . very nice.
SnowAngel:	do u think it's 2 much that i said "love"? cuz i DO love him. but i don't wanna scare him off. especially when he's already feeling guilty. i don't wanna, u know, overwhelm him.
zoegirl:	don't take this the wrong way, but r u absolutely positive

Send   Cancel

	u wanna send it? maybe u should just, u know, give it some time.
SnowAngel:	what good would that do? anyway, i already DID send it.
SnowAngel:	why, do u think i shouldn't have?
zoegirl:	i didn't say that
SnowAngel:	oh god, u think i shouldn't have sent it.
SnowAngel:	u think i'm a freak, don't u? is HE gonna think i'm a freak? oh no, this is terrible!
zoegirl:	hold on, angela. just wait and c what he says. there's nothing more u can do.
SnowAngel:	i could write him again. i could try to be more low-key!
zoegirl:	NO, angela. just wait and c.
SnowAngel:	right. ok.
SnowAngel:	anyway, i know ur, like, all worried, and that's really sweet of u. but i think it'll all work out. i just have a feeling.
SnowAngel:	in fact, i'm gonna go check my email in case he's already responded. BYE!

Monday, October 4, 10:51 PM

SnowAngel:	zoe?
zoegirl:	yeah?
SnowAngel:	he didn't write back.
zoegirl:	oh, angela
SnowAngel:	but maybe he hasn't had time to check his account. maybe he's been super busy.
zoegirl:	maybe so

Send   Cancel

ttyl

SnowAngel:	well . . . good nite
SnowAngel:	i'll check 1st thing in the morning and tell u what he says!!!

Tuesday, October 5, 10:01 PM

SnowAngel:	zoe, i need u!
zoegirl:	i'm here, i'm here. what happened?
SnowAngel:	I HATE TONNIE WYNDHAM!!! *clomps about in a flying rage*
zoegirl:	angela, what happened?
SnowAngel:	i called rob—just to talk, cuz he never did email me back last nite and in french he was all weird—and he hemmed and hawed and asked if we could do this l8r.
zoegirl:	"can we do this l8r"? that's what he said?
SnowAngel:	he said he was in the middle of a game of taboo. i was kinda hurt, but i was like, "sure, whatever." and then over the phone i heard this voice whining, "robbbbb, it's ur turn!" TONNIE WYNDHAM WAS AT HIS HOUSE!!! THEY WERE PLAYING TABOO TOGETHER!!!
zoegirl:	NO. WAY. what a loser.
SnowAngel:	i know! i HATE her!!!
zoegirl:	actually, i meant rob.
SnowAngel:	it's not his fault, tho. she probably just showed up unannounced. he doesn't know how to say no to her, remember?
zoegirl:	angela, r u even hearing yourself? ROB IS A LOSER!
SnowAngel:	but he's so cute! and i miss him so much!
zoegirl:	yeah, but he's treating u like dirt.

Send   Cancel

88

SnowAngel:	he is?
zoegirl:	he IS
SnowAngel:	oh
SnowAngel:	well then i'm not gonna call him back! i was going to, just to let him apologize, cuz i'm sure he feels really shitty. but he'll just have to call me himself!
zoegirl:	good for u
SnowAngel:	yeah. we'll c how he likes that, huh?
SnowAngel:	thanks, zoe. ur the best!

Tuesday, October 5, 10:12 PM

zoegirl:	omg, maddie. i just did it. i just told angela what a loser rob is and that she has to get over him!
mad maddie:	**ooo, way to be tough. did she listen?**
zoegirl:	i don't know. but maybe?
mad maddie:	**yay, zoe. WAY TO GO!**

Wednesday, October 6, 5:33 PM

SnowAngel:	hi, maddie. i've made up my mind: i'm gonna stop letting this rob business tear me up.
mad maddie:	**for real?**
SnowAngel:	cuz it's just stupid, right? why should i waste my life pining after him when all it's gonna do is make me miserable?
mad maddie:	**whoa—now ur talking. good for u, angela.**
SnowAngel:	so as soon as i get off the computer, i'm gonna bike over to his house so we can finally just talk and get it all out.
mad maddie:	**ANGELA!!! i thought u meant**

Send   Cancel

mad maddie:	**never mind. but didn't u already talk and get it all out, that day in french?**
SnowAngel:	no, cuz that's when he thought we weren't gonna be together anymore, which is ridiculous. i mean talk it out in a good way, so we can work out all our problems.
mad maddie:	**so ur going over there right now? ur just gonna show up on his doorstep?**
SnowAngel:	yeah, cuz then he can't turn me away.
mad maddie:	**er . . . doesn't that tell u something?**
SnowAngel:	i've g2g before i wimp out. bye!

Wednesday, October 6, 5:47 PM

mad maddie:	**shake a leg, zo. up and at 'em.**
zoegirl:	huh?
mad maddie:	**angela is biking over to rob's. she's gonna make him talk things out once and for all.**
zoegirl:	oh god
mad maddie:	**so get your mom to drop u off at her house. say u've gotta help her with her math or something.**
zoegirl:	i'll never get there in time. she'll have left already!
mad maddie:	**yeah, but we'll be there when she gets back.**
zoegirl:	ohhhhh
mad maddie:	**we're the ones who have to pick up the pieces. isn't that what u said a long time ago?**
zoegirl:	did i?
mad maddie:	**so c'mon, let's go!**

Thursday, October 7, 4:01 PM

zoegirl:	hey, angela. u doing any better today? u ran off after 6th period before i could find u!
SnowAngel:	2 busy crying. go away!
zoegirl:	but . . . ur on the computer. u can't be THAT busy.
SnowAngel:	yeah, well, i keep hoping rob will IM me or email or something, and that he'll tell me it was all a big mistake. that tonnie was talking out of her ass, and that the only reason he didn't tell her to shut up was cuz he's 2 nice of a guy.
SnowAngel:	pathetic, i know
zoegirl:	i don't think he's going to, angela.
SnowAngel:	i said I KNOW! god!
zoegirl:	ok
zoegirl:	well, if u wanna talk u know where to find me!

Thursday, October 7, 4:30 PM

mad maddie:	**hey, zo. have u checked on angela?**
zoegirl:	she's a mess. she didn't wanna talk to me.
mad maddie:	**she wouldn't talk to me, either. i called her on her cell, but she was all pissy.**
zoegirl:	it's like she's mad at us for being right.
mad maddie:	**i know. it's stupid.**
zoegirl:	i think she skipped french 2, cuz she didn't wanna deal with seeing rob. and i'm glad we ate lunch in the courtyard, cuz kristin said he and tonnie were all lovey-dovey during lunch.
mad maddie:	**yeah, she told me. don't they have any respect?**
zoegirl:	obviously not

zoegirl:	well, at least now she knows.
mad maddie:	**uh, yeah. i'd say the run-in at rob's house probably did the trick. what was it tonnie said when angela confronted them? "u brought it on yourself by being so blind"?**
zoegirl:	as if angela should have read the signs and figured it out herself, without rob having to spell it out.
mad maddie:	**altho the signs WERE there. i mean, WE knew.**
zoegirl:	still, rob is a total wimp. it's basically like he had tonnie break up with angela for him, which is incredibly lame.
mad maddie:	**oh well. u win some, u lose some. i just hope angela gets out of her funk before tomorrow, cuz in only 7 ½ short hours . . .**
zoegirl:	u turn 16! wh-hoo!!!
mad maddie:	**u got it, sport. byeas!**

Friday, October 8, 4:00 PM

zoegirl:	hey, angela. r u ready for maddie's party?
SnowAngel:	we've got almost an hour before we're supposed to be there, zoe.
zoegirl:	i know, but i'm so excited! aren't u?
zoegirl:	megan just called to get directions, and she really thinks maddie has no clue.
SnowAngel:	maybe. i dunno.
zoegirl:	angela! snap out of it. this is MADDIE'S PARTY, remember?
SnowAngel:	i'm just . . . i'm not really in the party mood.
zoegirl:	so get in the party mood. forget rob and forget tonnie. r they really more important than your best friend's

Send   Cancel

	party?
SnowAngel:	*flutters fingers lethargically in air*
zoegirl:	so r u dressed, at least? what r u gonna wear?
SnowAngel:	ur just asking to cheer me up. ur trying to distract me.
zoegirl:	no, i really wanna know.
SnowAngel:	*sighs*
SnowAngel:	mermaid print shirt, faded levis, maddie's bottlecap belt, brown leather clogs. scent: vanilla musk.
zoegirl:	that sounds so cute! i bet u look TERRIFIC.
SnowAngel:	oh, and my blue old navy hoodie tied around my waist, in case it gets chilly.
zoegirl:	excellent idea
SnowAngel:	u know, i really DO need this tonite. after my hell week, i mean. i just need to get out and be with u guys.
zoegirl:	god, i hear u. oh, and check this out. mr. h asked what my plans were this weekend. did i tell u?
SnowAngel:	he DID?
zoegirl:	after english, after everyone else left the room. is that weird?
SnowAngel:	i dunno. a little, maybe.
SnowAngel:	what did u say?
zoegirl:	that we were having a surprise party for maddie. he asked if boys were coming, and i said no. then he got this funny look on his face and said, "good."
SnowAngel:	what does THAT mean?
zoegirl:	that he doesn't want me lured away by some sophomore hottie, cuz he wants me for himself? jk

SnowAngel:	shit, zoe, i bet that's exactly what it meant.
zoegirl:	i said i was KIDDING.
SnowAngel:	i mean it. he's flirting with u.
zoegirl:	u really think so?
SnowAngel:	u better be careful, that's all i'm saying. take it from me: MEN SUCK.
zoegirl:	well, not ALL men.
SnowAngel:	hey, i've g2g, cuz i'm thinking maybe i'll change into something fancier, like my funky silk shirt. it IS a party, after all.
zoegirl:	that's my girl. c u soon!!!

Saturday, October 9, 11:14 AM

mad maddie:	**red hot! our team is red hot! our team is R-E-D! H-O-T! And once we start we can't be stopped! goooooooooo team!**
SnowAngel:	maddie?
mad maddie:	**thank u guys SO MUCH for my surprise party!!!! U R AWESOME!!!!!**
SnowAngel:	well i swan, madigan kinnick doing a girly-girl cheer. *fans self and calls for smelling salts*
mad maddie:	**i wouldn't do it for just anyone—just for my 2 best buds in the whole wide world. goooooooooo, team!**
SnowAngel:	were u really and truly surprised?
mad maddie:	**i was. it was perfect. and i was so glad that u were back among the living. i was really gonna have to hate u if u were a sourpuss on my big day.**
SnowAngel:	well, thanks, i guess. last nite was great, but this morning i woke up missing rob again. i still am really sad.

Send   Cancel

mad maddie:	**i know, i know**
mad maddie:	**but i have to run, cuz the pops is blaring the horn for me to get my fanny to the car. bday brunch, u know.**
SnowAngel:	well, try to have fun. and have fun at work tonite!
mad maddie:	**i will. hey, i'll try calling zo from my cell, but just in case, will u tell her thank u?**
SnowAngel:	u bet
mad maddie:	**byeas!**
SnowAngel:	bye, bday girl!!!

Sunday, October 10, 1:12 PM

mad maddie:	**hey, zoe**
zoegirl:	hey, mads
mad maddie:	**i have big news, big big big. which do u wanna hear first: maddie and ian get down and dirty OR maddie scores one for the gipper?**
zoegirl:	ooo, give me the down and dirty.
mad maddie:	**let me first just say that i would have told u this earlier, like at the crack of dawn when i called our dear friend angela.**
zoegirl:	the "crack of dawn" being what, around 10:30?
mad maddie:	**but noooooo, u weren't there to take my call, cuz u were off being holy with mr. h.**
zoegirl:	i'm here now, so spill it!
mad maddie:	**i dunno. u church types might find what i'm about to say offensive . . .**
zoegirl:	maddie? i swear i'm gonna get off-line if u don't tell me now. i'll get off-line AND take the phone off the hook.

mad maddie:	hmm. i suppose i'll take pity on u, since i'm older and wiser and know how foolish u youngsters can be.
zoegirl:	TELL ME!
mad maddie:	well there we were, me and ian. we'd gotten off work at around 11, but instead of going anywhere, we decided to hang out in my car—doesn't that have a nice ring? hang out in my car?—and listen to music.
zoegirl:	grooving in the gremlin. nice.
mad maddie:	ian had some watered-down rum and coke left over from a party he'd gone to on friday, and before u get all freaky on me, NO, i didn't have any. well, maybe a sip.
zoegirl:	maddie! u JUST got your license. u cannot drink and drive!!!
mad maddie:	a sip, zoe. i barely got my lips wet. ian drank the rest of it, which wasn't that much, but it was enuff to, like, loosen him up a little.
zoegirl:	and???
mad maddie:	and it was fun
mad maddie:	it was funny, actually, cuz even with the rum and coke, he was totally shy. he put his arm around me and shifted so that i was leaning against him, my back to his chest, but all he did was kiss the top of my head over and over.
zoegirl:	that's sweet!
mad maddie:	so we didn't really get down and dirty. we got . . . smudged. but it's a start, right?
zoegirl:	absolutely
mad maddie:	and u know what's really awesome? the fact that he goes to a different school.

Send   Cancel

zoegirl:	huh?
mad maddie:	**i know, it's weird. but it's like i can be whoever i wanna be around him, cuz i don't know shit about his school and he doesn't know shit about mine. so it's like none of that garbage gets in the way.**
zoegirl:	what garbage? like jana, u mean?
mad maddie:	**well, yeah, altho i don't mean just jana. and anywayz, she's not as bad as i thought. but ALL that stuff, all the cliques and hierarchies and in-crowds and out-crowds—i don't have to deal with it when i'm with ian.**
zoegirl:	sounds nice
mad maddie:	**it is**
mad maddie:	**and now r u ready for maddie scores one for the gipper?**
zoegirl:	who the hell is "the gipper"?
mad maddie:	**i have no idea. some football coach? but in this case it's u and angela.**
zoegirl:	i'm the gipper? all right. how'd u score one for me?
mad maddie:	**u AND angela, i said. cuz during brunch yesterday i bit the bullet and talked to my parents about letting us go to cumberland island.**
zoegirl:	and what'd they say?
mad maddie:	**i told them all about it, how it's only 5 hours away and how we wouldn't do any driving once we got there cuz we'd be camping out on the island, which we'd have to take a ferry to get to. i told them about all the research i'd done on the net, which made me sound extremely mature and industrious. i even printed up maps to show them. AND i said we might get to c wild horses, which would be, like, an experience of a lifetime.**

Send   Cancel

ttyl

zoegirl:	wow. r there really wild horses?
mad maddie:	**yeah, isn't that cool?**
mad maddie:	**so anywayz, i told the rents all of this, nodding very calmly and answering their questions, and when we were done talking, they looked at each other and said they'd think about it!!!**
zoegirl:	that's awesome!
mad maddie:	**so now it's up to u and angela. u've got to get going with your parents!**
zoegirl:	yeah, ok. email me some of that info, the maps and stuff.
mad maddie:	**tell them to at least consider it. don't let them give u an answer right away.**
zoegirl:	good plan
mad maddie:	**l8rs, gators!**

Monday, October 11, 7:42 PM

SnowAngel:	hey, mads. don't yell at me, ok?
mad maddie:	**what r u talking about?**
SnowAngel:	i called rob. i just wanted to hear his voice.
mad maddie:	**angela!!!**
SnowAngel:	but i hung up when he answered. i just didn't know what to say.
SnowAngel:	aren't u gonna respond?
mad maddie:	**oh. well, that's ok then.**
mad maddie:	**sorry if i'm taking a while to answer, but i've got, like, 3 other IMs going.**
SnowAngel:	with who?
SnowAngel:	never mind. just tell them u've gotta go cuz your best

Send   Cancel

	friend is having a crisis
SnowAngel:	r u there?!!
mad maddie:	**so u called rob, which was bad. but u hung up before u actually talked to him, which is good. even tho it makes u kinda like a stalker.**
SnowAngel:	except then i got worried that he'd *69 me, so i called right back.
mad maddie:	**ANGELA!**
SnowAngel:	i was all, "that was so weird! i just called u, but u never answered. is there something wrong with your phone?"
mad maddie:	**u asked if there was something wrong with his phone?!!**
SnowAngel:	well, there could have been! phones go screwy all the time.
SnowAngel:	u don't think he thought i was making it up, do u?
mad maddie:	**why no, angela. why on earth would he think that?**
SnowAngel:	anyway, i hoped . . . i dunno. i hoped that when he heard my voice, he'd remember all the fun we'd had and he'd want to get back together. but there was just this really long silence, and then he said, "so, did u want something?"
SnowAngel:	MADDIE!!!
mad maddie:	**i'm here, sorry**
mad maddie:	**and all i can say is, rob's an asshole**
SnowAngel:	i know, but i miss him anyway. it just hurts, maddie. ⊗
SnowAngel:	why do these things always happen to ME?
mad maddie:	**that is a very good question.**
SnowAngel:	well, good-bye. i suppose i'll go watch "7th heaven."

	waves hankerchief forlornly
mad maddie:	**good idea. AND STAY AWAY FROM THE PHONE!!!**

Monday, October 11, 7:56 PM

SnowAngel:	i miss rob 🙁
zoegirl:	i know. poor angela.
SnowAngel:	do u think i should call him? i called him once already—actually twice—but our convo was kinda weird. maybe i should call him again to straighten things out.
zoegirl:	i don't know, angela. maybe u should just wait and talk to him at school.
SnowAngel:	but he never does talk to me! he practically runs down the hall every time he sees me!
zoegirl:	well, doesn't that tell u something?
zoegirl:	i don't mean to be harsh
SnowAngel:	fine. screw him. HE'S the one missing out, not me.
zoegirl:	so true. be strong!

Tuesday, October 12, 5:23 PM

| SnowAngel: | maddie, u r in big trouble! it was downright chilly walking home from school today—i'm talking serious nipple weather—but i guess u wouldn't know since u were snug and warm IN YOUR CAR. did u sneak off to meet ian? hmm? is that why u forgot to pick me up, cuz u wanted some more of his sweet loving? |
| **mad maddie:** | **Angela? This is Madigan's mother. My account is down, and I needed to check on one of my bids on eBay.** |

Send   Cancel

100

SnowAngel:	oh, ok. i'm really sorry.
mad maddie:	**Is there something I should know about Madigan and Ian?**
SnowAngel:	no! i was just joking around. i'll get off now, ok?
mad maddie:	**ha ha, gotcha.**
SnowAngel:	shit, maddie! *tries to stop hyperventilating*
mad maddie:	**don't worry, the moms could never log on as me. she doesn't know my password.**
SnowAngel:	U SUCK!!!
mad maddie:	**did u like the correct punctuation, tho? that was a nice touch, i think.**
SnowAngel:	u r a total freak and i hate u.
SnowAngel:	so why DID u forget me?! i waited for 20 minutes and u never showed up!
mad maddie:	**wait a minute, chickie. i was there at 4 o'clock sharp. U were the one who didn't show.**
SnowAngel:	what? i stopped by the auditorium to find out about drama club sign-up, and then i came right to the parking lot.
mad maddie:	**well, sorry. i'd told jana i'd give her a ride 2, and she kinda wanted to get going.**
SnowAngel:	EXCUSE me?
mad maddie:	**i ran into her after 7th period. she lives sorta near me, u know.**
SnowAngel:	omg. i can't believe u ditched me to give jana whitaker a ride.
mad maddie:	**don't have a cow. god.**
SnowAngel:	well, think about it, maddie. first u treat jana like

	she's the anti-christ, and now all of a sudden—snap!—ur her chauffeur? and not only that, but ur driving HER instead of ME?
mad maddie:	**angela, u live 5 blocks from school. u walk home every day of your life.**
SnowAngel:	that is so not the point and u know it.
mad maddie:	**she needed a ride**
SnowAngel:	and out of all the ppl in the world, U had to give her one?
mad maddie:	**not that many sophomores have cars. i do.**
SnowAngel:	omg, ur a car snob! u've had your license for four days and ur already a car snob!
mad maddie:	**this is stupid. do u have anything important to say, or did u just wanna rag on me some more?**
SnowAngel:	*lifts eyebrows*
mad maddie:	**whatevs. i'm outta here.**
SnowAngel:	fine!

Tuesday, October 12, 5:45 PM

SnowAngel:	zoe? thank god.
zoegirl:	hey, angela. what's up?
SnowAngel:	i am so pissed at maddie. she is so annoying! 😩
zoegirl:	why? what happened?
SnowAngel:	she gave jana whitaker a ride home instead of me. can u believe that? i was 10 minutes late getting to the parking lot, and she left without me!
zoegirl:	well, at least u live close to school.
SnowAngel:	but zoe! she left cuz jana told her to, and

Send   Cancel

	then she acted like it was totally no big deal. like it was my problem for getting bent out of shape.
zoegirl:	hmm
SnowAngel:	it's jana. she's buddying up to maddie and making her feel cool, and maddie's totally falling for it. it's sickening. 😞😞😞
zoegirl:	maybe jana had an appointment or something. maybe she had to get home by a certain time.
SnowAngel:	that makes no sense. if jana had anything important to get to, her mom would have picked her up, not maddie.
zoegirl:	i guess. yeah, ur right.
zoegirl:	hey, wanna come with me to the junkman's daughter?
SnowAngel:	isn't that a thrift shop? u know i have polyester issues, zoe.
zoegirl:	i just want a good pair of jeans, some really soft, beat-up ones.
SnowAngel:	what for?
zoegirl:	uh . . . to wear? i'm going to a wellspring party this friday. mr. h is gonna be there.
SnowAngel:	ohhhhhhh. sure, i'll come.
SnowAngel:	at least i know u'll actually show, unlike SOME ppl i know.
zoegirl:	my mom's pretty much ready to go, so we'll pick u up in 15 minutes. bye!

Thursday, October 14, 10:02 PM

SnowAngel:	oh, man. oh man, oh man, oh man.

zoegirl:	hi, angela. "oh man" what?
SnowAngel:	u know how i said i needed a distraction to help me get over rob? well, welcome to recovery, baby, cuz distraction has arrived.
zoegirl:	does this mean—let me just make a wild guess here—that u've found a new crush?
SnowAngel:	it is SUCH a relief to be moving on, i can't even tell u.
zoegirl:	who's the lucky fella?
SnowAngel:	his name's ben. ☺ he's helping out with drama club, and i swear, zo, he is every kinda hot.
zoegirl:	oh yeah?
SnowAngel:	*drools* i think about rob now, and i don't know what i ever saw in him. i mean, sometimes i even wonder if i was just in luv with the idea of being in luv, u know?
zoegirl:	u don't say
SnowAngel:	but ben. *sigh* he's a drama major at georgia state, and he's getting course credit for being our assistant director. he's got curly brown hair and gorgeous brown eyes, and he's got the tiniest bit of a pot belly, but on him it's really cute.
zoegirl:	nice
SnowAngel:	but u wanna know what i really like about him? how intense he is—like he's thinking all these profound thoughts. god, he's so much more mature than high school guys.
zoegirl:	is he gonna work with u for the whole semester?
SnowAngel:	uh huh. he talked to us today about the play we're putting on—which is The Crucible—and he said that creating art is the most important thing we can ever

Send   Cancel

	do. it was so inspiring.
zoegirl:	that's awesome. r u trying out for an actual role?
SnowAngel:	hell no, i signed up to do makeup. but that's art 2, zoe.
zoegirl:	i know, i know. i think that's great.
SnowAngel:	i'm soooooooo excited. it feels good to have something to be psyched about, u know?
zoegirl:	have u told maddie?
SnowAngel:	no
zoegirl:	why not? ur not still mad at her, r u?
SnowAngel:	c'mon. u saw her today, laffing 2 loudly at everything jana said. and i HATE that new expression she has.
zoegirl:	"tits," u mean?
SnowAngel:	me: "so maddie, what'd ya think of that geometry test?" maddie: "tits, man. i totally aced it." *rolls eyes and vomits*
zoegirl:	yeah. i called her an hour ago to talk about our piano lessons, cuz mrs. lynch is out of town. i asked if she'd gotten the message, and she was like, "so i don't have to go to my lesson? tits!"
SnowAngel:	it's so embarrassing. have u heard jana call her "the madster" yet?
zoegirl:	oh, no!
SnowAngel:	and maddie calls her "the janster." *vomits some more*
zoegirl:	ack
SnowAngel:	at least she hasn't invited jana on our road trip— which actually is kinda amazing.
zoegirl:	oh, baloney. jana may be the flavor of the week, but

	maddie knows who her real friends r.
SnowAngel:	i hope so
SnowAngel:	speaking of the road trip, i sort of broached the topic with my mom, just in a breezy, chatty kinda way, and she said it sounded fun. now i just have to tell her that we seriously wanna go—not hypothetically, but for real.
zoegirl:	that's pretty much where i am 2.
zoegirl:	actually, that's not true. i keep MEANING to bring it up, but then i get scared about mom's reaction and i wimp out.
SnowAngel:	zoe! u HAVE to. thanksgiving break's not that far away!
zoegirl:	i know, i know
SnowAngel:	did u wash your new jeans, get rid of that funky smell?
zoegirl:	i did. they're perfect. i thought about patching the hole in the knee, but i decided not to.
SnowAngel:	sexy miss zoe, stepping out in her sexy new jeans. *prances down the catwalk*
zoegirl:	shut up. i just wanna look decent, that's all. not all nerdy like i normally do.
SnowAngel:	u don't look nerdy!
zoegirl:	well, boring then. i definitely look boring.
zoegirl:	hey, wanna come home with me tomorrow and do my makeup for the wellspring party?
SnowAngel:	u mean it?! ur finally gonna let me give u a makeover? *jumps up and down and squeals*
zoegirl:	only if u promise not to go crazy.
SnowAngel:	ooo, this is gonna be fabulous. i luv makeup. ☺

Send   Cancel

zoegirl:	that's why i finally decided to ask, cuz u always seem so happy when ur doing your own. i watched u put on your blush last weekend, and u couldn't stop smiling.
SnowAngel:	???
SnowAngel:	ohhhh, i know what ur talking about. that was so i'd apply my blush right, u goof. when u smile, it makes it easier to find the apples of your cheeks.
zoegirl:	oh. i just thought u were really happy.
SnowAngel:	i AM really happy—that i get to do yours. i'll make u a star, baby.
zoegirl:	er . . .
SnowAngel:	i'm signing off so u don't have time to wimp out. bye!

Friday, October 15, 4:54 PM

mad maddie:	**zo-ster!**
zoegirl:	hey, mads. what's up?
mad maddie:	**well, i'm sorry to report that i've discovered a smell worse than period farts.**
zoegirl:	period farts?
mad maddie:	**don't play dumb. i'm talking about those wretched farts u get when u have your period, which r totally different from normal farts?**
zoegirl:	ahem, maddie? i don't like where this is going.
mad maddie:	**me neither, and i should know cuz i'm the one who—for some INSANE reason—agreed to try mark's disgusting soy milk with my raisin bran this morning.**
zoegirl:	ew. i didn't know anyone actually drank that stuff.
mad maddie:	**pelt-woman does. she says it's good for your brain. and now mark does 2, cuz he has to do everything**

Send   Cancel

	she does. i wish he would hurry up and move into his own apartment and take his nasty soy milk with him, cuz DAMN is it gross. u have to shake it before u use it, and sometimes little clots of bean curd come floating out.
zoegirl:	that is revolting
mad maddie:	**and now i have the nastiest gas i've ever had in my life. AND i've got a "date" with ian tonite. i'm trying to get it all out now before he picks me up.**
zoegirl:	a "date," huh? like, a date date?
mad maddie:	**dinner and a movie, the whole shebang.**
zoegirl:	maddie, that's so sweet! u've got a real live beau!
mad maddie:	**until i blow him away with my farts, that is.**
mad maddie:	**hey, if i IM angela, is she gonna act all pissy, or has she forgiven me for giving jana a ride home on monday?**
zoegirl:	she's still annoyed, but u should IM her anyway. she was just over here, but i bet she's home by now.
mad maddie:	**why was she over there? were u guys having a secret powwow w/o me?**
zoegirl:	relax, she was just teaching me how to do makeup. u would've hated it.
mad maddie:	**that's for damn sure**
mad maddie:	**anyway, the whole jana thing was SO not a big deal. angela made it out like i was picking jana over her, and that totally wasn't the case.**
zoegirl:	listen, u don't have to convince me.
mad maddie:	**i mean, u and angela r my best friends, that goes without saying. but that doesn't mean i can't be friends with jana 2.**

Send   Cancel

zoegirl:	i'm really ok with this, maddie.
mad maddie:	**right. sorry.**
mad maddie:	**so . . . what r u doing tonite? any big plans now that ur all made up and beautiful?**
zoegirl:	tonite? nah. i'll be psyched to hear how your date goes, tho.
mad maddie:	**yeah, i'll tell u all about it. guess i better—oops, there goes another one.**
zoegirl:	another what?
mad maddie:	**another soy milk fart. my butt cheeks r still flapping. byeas!**

Friday, October 15, 5:55 PM

mad maddie:	**hola, angela. r u still mad at me, or have u realized the error of your ways?**
SnowAngel:	???
mad maddie:	**never mind. let's talk about something else, like my date with ian. i'm actually kinda nervous. isn't that weird?**
SnowAngel:	no. that means u like him!
mad maddie:	**i keep wondering if he'll be more aggressive tonite, if he'll go for the gusto and kiss me on the lips and not just the top of my head.**
SnowAngel:	do u want him to?
mad maddie:	**i think so, yeah.**
SnowAngel:	first kisses r sooooooo romantic. *sighs*
mad maddie:	**what about u? what r u up to tonite?**
SnowAngel:	NOTHING! *stomps around and kicks things* i feel like such a loser.
mad maddie:	**that sucks**

SnowAngel:	tell me about it. altho it's not SO bad, cuz Maid in Manhattan is on TBS at 8:00. i luv that movie.
mad maddie:	**tits, man**
SnowAngel:	will u PLEASE stop saying that? that is the dumbest expression i've ever heard. it's like saying, "penis, man," or "testicles. awesome."
mad maddie:	**ooo—aren't we touchy**
mad maddie:	**anyway, u should call zo, tell her to come watch Maid in Manhattan with u.**
SnowAngel:	well, yeah, if she didn't have her own hot date. thanks for rubbing it in.
mad maddie:	**zoe has a date?**
SnowAngel:	fine, so it's not technically a "date." it's still more exciting than popcorn and tv.
mad maddie:	**exsqueeze me, but what r u talking about?**
SnowAngel:	that wellspring party zoe's going to. get with the program.
mad maddie:	**zoe's going to a wellspring party? tonite?**
SnowAngel:	r we having a communication problem here? *cups hands around mouth* YES, ZOE'S GOING TO A WELLSPRING PARTY TONITE. that's why she got those new jeans she was wearing today, and that's why i went over and dolled her up. she looks totally fab, btw.
mad maddie:	**hold on. i IMed zoe like 10 minutes ago, and she said nothing about a wellspring party. i asked her flat-out what she was doing tonite, and she didn't say a word.**
SnowAngel:	huh. probably cuz she didn't want u saying, "tits, man."
mad maddie:	**screw u. is mr. h gonna be there?**
SnowAngel:	he's the one who told her about it.

Send   Cancel

mad maddie: **what?!!**

mad maddie: **all right, fine. i can't think about this anymore.**

SnowAngel: wait a minute—r u upset about this?

mad maddie: **don't be dumb**

SnowAngel: cuz u seem upset, and now i'm thinking i shouldn't have said anything.

mad maddie: **ian's gonna be here soon. i've g2g.**

SnowAngel: ok, if u say so. have fun!

Saturday, October 16, 11:03 AM

zoegirl: angela! oh, AN-gela!

SnowAngel: hey hey hey! how was the party?

zoegirl: well . . . fun, kinda. billy summers brought his guitar, and we did a lot of sing-a-longs. maddie would have laffed her head off.

SnowAngel: what about mr. h? was he there?

zoegirl: he was

SnowAngel: and?

zoegirl: ack. i really should tell u in person. r u still coming over?

SnowAngel: don't u DARE leave me hanging like that. did something happen with mr. h?!!!

zoegirl: i don't know. maybe?

SnowAngel: TELL ME!!!!

zoegirl: well . . . it was when he gave me a ride home. i was about to call my mom to pick me up, but he said he was ready to go 2.

SnowAngel: i bet

zoegirl: so it was just the 2 of us in his car, and at first i felt pretty jumpy. i don't know why, really, except maybe

	that it was dark out? it made things feel more intimate than the times he took me to church.
SnowAngel:	mmm-hmmm. go on.
zoegirl:	so . . . we talked. and when we got to my house, he cut the engine and we talked a little longer. which shows how innocent it was, cuz my parents were right there, less than 20 feet away.
SnowAngel:	yeah, INSIDE the house
zoegirl:	he said i seem a lot older than 15, and that he's really enjoyed getting to know me. i know it sounds corny, but it was nice.
SnowAngel:	i can c that
zoegirl:	and then . . .
SnowAngel:	what?
zoegirl:	well, he made this comment about my jeans, teasing me about how raggedy they were. and then he reached over and touched the hole, kinda running his finger around the worn part.
SnowAngel:	zoe! OMG!!!
zoegirl:	it was almost like he was doing it as an excuse to touch my leg.
SnowAngel:	well, yeah! cuz he WAS doing it as an excuse to touch your leg!
zoegirl:	but he wasn't being a lech or anything. i don't want u to get the wrong idea.
SnowAngel:	shit, zoe. HE'S YOUR TEACHER!!!
zoegirl:	i know
SnowAngel:	did u like it? ooo—that sounds icky. i mean, was it ok with u that he did that?

Send   Cancel

zoegirl:	i don't know. i'm not mad or anything, if that's what u mean.
SnowAngel:	*whistles*
zoegirl:	do u think that's awful? do u think it's really gross?
SnowAngel:	r u still gonna go to church with him on sunday?
zoegirl:	uh huh. my mom's baking thumbprint cookies to give him when he picks me up, the kind with jam inside. she, like, adores him.
SnowAngel:	wow
zoegirl:	don't tell anyone any of this, all right? i mean, i know u wouldn't, but i just wanted to make sure.
SnowAngel:	don't worry
SnowAngel:	even if i did, no one would believe me.
zoegirl:	what's that supposed to mean?
SnowAngel:	just that ur so pure and innocent. no one would believe that ur secretly this lady of the nite.
zoegirl:	angela!
SnowAngel:	jk
zoegirl:	NOT funny
SnowAngel:	so what time u want me to come over? i can come right now if u want.
zoegirl:	sure. and hopefully maddie'll drop by after work, if she doesn't stay after with ian.
SnowAngel:	mmm—maybe she'll bring some beignets. c ya!

Send   Cancel

Sunday, October 17, 6:32 PM

zoegirl: maddie—FINALLY!

mad maddie: what?

zoegirl: i've called half a dozen times, and u never called back. AND u never stopped by last nite. 2 busy with ian?

mad maddie: not really. we hung out a little, but i was home by 11:30.

zoegirl: so why didn't u come over?

mad maddie: guess it slipped my mind. woops.

zoegirl: oh. well, that's ok. DID u have fun with ian?

mad maddie: it was all right

zoegirl: that's all? just all right?

mad maddie: yep

zoegirl: oh. so . . . what r u doing now?

mad maddie: nothing

zoegirl: ok-a-a-a-y

zoegirl: is something wrong, maddie?

mad maddie: should there be?

zoegirl: no, it's just . . . u don't really seem into this, that's all.

mad maddie: well, sorry to disappoint u. guess u'll have to IM angela instead.

zoegirl: huh?

mad maddie: she's the one u confide in, after all.

zoegirl: what? maddie, i have no idea what ur talking about!

mad maddie: right. of course. so how was YOUR weekend?

zoegirl: it was fine. we missed u, tho.

mad maddie: i bet. what about friday nite? u miss me then?

Send   Cancel

zoegirl:	crap, maddie. is THAT what this is about?
mad maddie:	me: so what r u up to tonite? u: oh, nothing.
mad maddie:	god, zoe, u lied to my face!
zoegirl:	maddie . . .
mad maddie:	why did u tell angela and not me?
zoegirl:	truthfully? cuz i knew u'd make fun of me, and i'm sick of it.
mad maddie:	u still should have told me. i HATE it when u and angela have your stupid little secrets.
zoegirl:	well, i'm sorry. i didn't mean to hurt your feelings.
mad maddie:	well, u did
zoegirl:	i'm sorry. i really am.
zoegirl:	maddie? r u still there?
mad maddie:	i'm here
zoegirl:	do u forgive me?
mad maddie:	no
mad maddie:	r u gonna tell me about it, at least?
zoegirl:	we sang jesus-loves-me songs. happy?
mad maddie:	what about mr. h? angela says that's why u got those new jeans, to get him all hot and bothered.
zoegirl:	i did not!
mad maddie:	did he jump your bones?
zoegirl:	c, maddie? this is the problem with talking to u about this. u act all offended if i DON'T tell u, but when i DO, all u can do is rag on me.
mad maddie:	i'm not ragging on u. i'm serious. one day he's gonna lure u away and lock u in a sex prison, i'm not kidding.

zoegirl:	i told u all there is to tell. we sang songs, cherryl ann booth gave a devotional, some of the kids played jeff's dad's pinball machine. the end.
mad maddie:	**sounds dull as nails**
zoegirl:	it was. and now i have to go, cuz even tho we went to the same party, i still have to do my homework for mr. h's class.
mad maddie:	**ooo, homework . . .**
zoegirl:	BYE, maddie!

Sunday, October 17, 7:15 PM

mad maddie:	**zoe? u still there?**
zoegirl:	yesssss. i was just about to log-off.
mad maddie:	**i just wanted to say—really quickly—that i DID have fun with ian. it was better than all right.**
zoegirl:	aw, maddie, that's great.
mad maddie:	**i didn't tell u at first cuz u were on my bad list. but then i started thinking, what if somehow ian saw what i said? not that he ever would. but what if he did, and he thought i wasn't into him?**
zoegirl:	how would he c?
mad maddie:	**he wouldn't. but that's the thing about the internet, it's just kinda spooky. i mean, everything's out there, u know?**
zoegirl:	ur paranoid. DON'T WORRY, IAN! MADDIE REALLY DOES LIKE U!
mad maddie:	**i just wanted to set the record straight. ok, byeas for real!**

Send   Cancel

Monday, October 18, 8:11 PM

SnowAngel:	hey, miss maddie-pie
mad maddie:	**hey, angela. how's tricks?**
SnowAngel:	just another day in sophomore paradise. *hums and floats about room*
mad maddie:	**would this have to do with drama club, per chance? old what's-his-name's made quite an impression, i c.**
SnowAngel:	his name's ben. *sighs* ben schlanker.
mad maddie:	**ben schlanker? as in schlong + wanker?**
SnowAngel:	oh god, maddie. please don't do this.
mad maddie:	**schlanker. that's hysterical. if u get married, u'll be angela schlanker.**
SnowAngel:	damn u. WHY do u plant these things in my head?!!
mad maddie:	**or i suppose u could hyphenate. then u'd be angela silver-schlanker.**
SnowAngel:	enuff about the name. *glares*
SnowAngel:	do u wanna hear how wonderful he is or not?
mad maddie:	**i'd rather make fun of his name some more.**
SnowAngel:	he's Jewish, maddie. "schlanker" is a nice, normal Jewish name. ur being kinda racist, u know.
mad maddie:	**sccchhlllanker. hahahahahahahahahahaha.**
SnowAngel:	ANYWAY, today ben told us that u have to claw to live, that suffering is what life is all about. isn't that cool?
mad maddie:	**u have to claw to live?**
SnowAngel:	he said suffering brings things into focus. most ppl just go la-la-la along their lives, he said, but artists have to stay sharp. we can't be afraid to embrace pain.

Send   Cancel

mad maddie:	so i suppose u'll be plucking eyebrows, then? applying lots of hot wax facials?
SnowAngel:	huh?
mad maddie:	well, ur the makeup girl. ur in a prime position to help the actors embrace as much pain as possible.
SnowAngel:	u just don't get it, do u? oh well. your loss.
mad maddie:	so does this ben guy even know your name?
SnowAngel:	YES he knows my name. god. today he said something about adam lancaster needing a scar, and he glanced at me and said, "which angela'll take care of, right angela?"
mad maddie:	does he have a girlfriend?
SnowAngel:	*growls*
mad maddie:	does that mean yes?
SnowAngel:	he talks about some leslie chick a lot. apparently she goes to GA State with him. but maybe she's just a friend. *crosses fingers* hey, i'm gonna take off, ok?
mad maddie:	sure. i told the moms i'd go to the drugstore for her, anywayz. l8rs!

Tuesday, October 19, 10:23 PM

mad maddie:	hola, zo-ster
zoegirl:	hey, mads
mad maddie:	i gave jana a ride home again today—don't tell angela.
zoegirl:	lovely
zoegirl:	so how is ol' jana?
mad maddie:	she's good. she cracks me up, all the crazy things she's done. she's actually been cow-tipping, can u believe that?

118

zoegirl:	no. where'd she find a cow in atlanta? and even if she did, that's mean.
mad maddie:	**it's not mean. it's funny. but anywayz, she has this awesome idea for how to make a statement about how dumb the speed limit is. wanna hear it?**
zoegirl:	i suppose
mad maddie:	**well, u know how EVERYONE drives over 65, right? which makes it totally pointless to even have a speed limit. i mean, seriously. we should be like germany where everyone just drives at their own speed.**
zoegirl:	that's jana's statement? be like germany?
mad maddie:	**hold your horses. here's her idea: we're gonna get a bunch of ppl to drive out to I-285. we'll have at least 5 cars, 1 for each lane, and we'll work it so that we're all right next to each other. then we'll set our speed at EXACTLY 65mph, all at the same time. we'll TOTALLY block traffic. won't that be awesome?!!**
zoegirl:	i don't get it. how will u block traffic by going 65mph?
mad maddie:	**cuz no one goes 65mph! but this time they'll have to, cuz no one will be able to pass us!**
zoegirl:	u've got to be kidding
zoegirl:	ur not actually gonna do this, r u?
mad maddie:	**hell, yeah. it's brilliant.**
zoegirl:	haven't u heard of road rage? ur gonna get shot!
mad maddie:	**that's ridiculous**
mad maddie:	**i knew angela would be all critical, but i thought u would get it, since u care about issues and stuff.**
zoegirl:	important issues, not rebelling against the speed limit.

Send   Cancel

119

mad maddie:	**whatevs. we're doing it this friday during rush hour if u wanna come.**
zoegirl:	have u heard anything i've just said? NO i don't wanna come. it makes me nervous just thinking about it.
mad maddie:	**yeah, isn't it great? that's what i love about jana. when i'm with her, i get this excitement inside of me and a "i'm ready to do anything" attitude. it scares the shit out of me.**
zoegirl:	and u like that?
mad maddie:	**i love it**
zoegirl:	weird
mad maddie:	**speaking of excitement—have u asked your parents about cumberland island yet? u keep saying ur gonna, and then u never do!**
zoegirl:	oh. didn't i tell u? i DID ask them, and they pretty much said no freakin way. mom's exact words were, "3 15-year-olds alone on the highway? r u out of your mind?"
mad maddie:	**hey! i'm 16!!!**
zoegirl:	i told her that. it didn't make any difference.
mad maddie:	**did u beg and plead and throw a fit?**
zoegirl:	they're not gonna go for it, mads. it sucks, but they're just not.
mad maddie:	**well, i'm gonna figure something out. i'm not giving up yet!**

Wednesday, October 20, 7:14 PM

mad maddie:	**i am on a hot streak. streak, i tell u, streak!**
SnowAngel:	oh, yeah? what's going on?

mad maddie: first set up that chat thing and let's get zoe in here. i wanna tell u both at the same time.

SnowAngel: ok, chat invite coming your way.

You have just entered the room "Angela's Boudoir."
madmaddie has entered the room.
zoegirl has entered the room.

SnowAngel: ta-da!

zoegirl: hey, angela. hey, mads. wazzup?

mad maddie: SO. i talked to the moms again about our cumberland island trip, and guess what she said?!!!

SnowAngel: what?

mad maddie: well . . . she and the pops don't think it's a good idea for us to go by ourselves, cuz she's worried we'd get a flat or pick up a hitchhiker or something. whatevs. so i said, "what if mark and erin came 2?" and she talked it over with dad, and they said YES!

zoegirl: erin? who's erin?

mad maddie: mark's girlfriend. pelt-woman. i made mark call her right then, and she thinks it's a great idea. wild horses, camping, remote little island—it's totally up her alley.

SnowAngel: maddie, that's AWESOME! ☺

zoegirl: it is. it totally is. but wouldn't it be weird, the 3 of us plus mark and erin?

mad maddie: no. we'll tail each other down there, but mark and erin'll have their own car and we'll have ours. and once we get to the island, we won't even have to c them. we can camp wherever we want, and so can they.

Send   Cancel

121

SnowAngel:	maddie, ur brilliant. now we just have to convince my parents and zoe's parents.
zoegirl:	oh, god. i'm gonna be the 1 person who doesn't get to go. i just know it.
mad maddie:	**talk to them tonite. remind them that mark and erin r both 18, and we'll be with them the whole time. we really won't, but they don't have to know that.**
SnowAngel:	true
mad maddie:	**and tell them they can call u on your cell whenever they want. we HAVE to make it happen, you guys. it's important. cuz sometimes i feel like we're drifting away from each other, and we can't let that happen.**
SnowAngel:	we r not drifting away from each other. what r u talking about?
SnowAngel:	if anyone's drifting away, it's U
mad maddie:	**wtf?**
zoegirl:	ur not drifting away, don't worry.
mad maddie:	**cuz i am the one person who has stayed exactly the same. u 2 r the ones changing, not me.**
SnowAngel:	hey, ur the 1 who brought it up, madster
mad maddie:	**christ, is THAT what this is about? i can't believe ur bringing that up again!**
SnowAngel:	neither can i, so just forget it. anyway, i have to ask u both something that doesn't have to do with our trip.
zoegirl:	shoot
SnowAngel:	wanna go bowling with me on friday? doug schmidt asked me to go, and i couldn't bear to turn him down. but i don't want it to be a date-type thing, so i told him i'd c if anyone else wanted to come 2.

Send   Cancel

zoegirl:	he wants to go BOWLING? that's so cute!
mad maddie:	**hold on. doug schmidt asked u out—for the forty millionth time—and u said, "sure, why don't i bring my friends along?"**
SnowAngel:	it's better than saying no, isn't it?
mad maddie:	**not much**
SnowAngel:	so do u wanna come? please, please, please?
mad maddie:	**can't, sorry**
SnowAngel:	why not?
mad maddie:	**i've got plans**
SnowAngel:	with ian?
mad maddie:	**with some ppl from school**
zoegirl:	oh, that's right. but that doesn't mean ur drifting away. it's just that she asked u 1st.
SnowAngel:	WHO asked u 1st?
SnowAngel:	omg. do u have plans with JANA?
mad maddie:	**thanks, zo**
zoegirl:	shit
SnowAngel:	*stomps foot* somebody better tell me RIGHT NOW what ur doing with jana!
zoegirl:	it's nothing. they're doing their hw together. right, mads?
mad maddie:	**give it up, loser. it's 2 late.**
mad maddie:	**we're not doing hw. we're just . . . we're doing this driving thing. it's no big deal.**
SnowAngel:	what kind of "driving thing"?
mad maddie:	**i'll tell u about it tomorrow. i'm getting off now.**
SnowAngel:	fine, just DON'T try to tell me ur not changing.

Send   Cancel

mad maddie:	**whatevs. ttyl!**

mad maddie has left the room.

SnowAngel:	god, what a grump
SnowAngel:	would u please tell me what that was all about?
zoegirl:	nothing. seriously. maddie'll explain it all tomorrow, and it really should be her who tells u. but it's not a big deal, i swear.
SnowAngel:	*sighs dramatically* whatever
SnowAngel:	so will U at least go with me and doug?
zoegirl:	uh . . . sure, i guess
SnowAngel:	yay! ur the best! BYE!

Thursday, October 21, 5:51 PM

zoegirl:	hey, angela. it's me.
SnowAngel:	zoe! i told doug ur coming with us on friday and he's psyched. 😊
zoegirl:	er . . . actually, that's why i IMed.
SnowAngel:	ur not having second thoughts, r u? ha ha
SnowAngel:	when doug heard u were coming, he said he'd ask steve brinks to come 2. it can be like a double-date.
zoegirl:	aaiee. i can't go after all, angela. don't hate me!
SnowAngel:	WHAT? i was kidding about the double-date, zo. doug really is gonna invite steve, but just as a friends thing.
zoegirl:	it's not that
SnowAngel:	then what?
zoegirl:	don't be mad, ok? it's just that i stayed for mr. h's

Send   Cancel

124

	backwork today, and he kinda asked if i wanted to play bingo with him on friday nite.
SnowAngel:	WHAT?!!!
zoegirl:	not just us—his mother'll be there 2. she lives in a nursing home, and once a month they have bingo nite. he asked if i wanted to go.
SnowAngel:	let me get this straight: ur ditching me to play bingo with mr. h and his mother?
zoegirl:	please don't hate me. it's just that i kinda forgot about our bowling plans til it was 2 late. and . . . i really wanna go.
SnowAngel:	i don't get it. how can mr. h ask u to go play bingo with him as if it's a totally normal thing? doesn't he know that ur his student?
zoegirl:	we'll be with a bunch of old ppl, angela. i think it's really sweet.
SnowAngel:	*shakes head* unbelievable
zoegirl:	he wants me to meet his mother. don't u think that's kinda a big deal?
SnowAngel:	i think it's kinda INSANE
SnowAngel:	have u told maddie?
zoegirl:	no, just u
SnowAngel:	good, cuz maddie would have a heyday.
zoegirl:	so . . . r u mad?
SnowAngel:	yes *sticks out tongue*
SnowAngel:	but i suppose i'll forgive u eventually.
zoegirl:	thank u, thank u, thank u
SnowAngel:	EVENTUALLY, i said. right now i'm gonna call megan and kristin and c if either of them can go. or maybe

Send   Cancel

	i'll IM maddie and tell her she has to forget that idiotic driving thing and be my escort since u turned traitor.
zoegirl:	she finally told u?
zoegirl:	that was so weird how at first she didn't want u to know.
SnowAngel:	i know. i totally don't get it. did she actually say "please don't tell angela"?
zoegirl:	pretty much
SnowAngel:	how annoying
zoegirl:	i mean, she gets all hurt if i tell u something and not her—like about that wellspring party—but she thinks it's fine to tell me stuff and not u.
SnowAngel:	so what was the deal, did she think i'd disapprove cuz it involved jana?
zoegirl:	something like that
SnowAngel:	well, i do, and that's even more reason she should bag it. anyway, i need her more than jana does.
SnowAngel:	think she'll listen?
zoegirl:	i have no idea. i'd try kristin or megan 1st, though.
SnowAngel:	i suppose. bye!

Thursday, October 21, 6:13 PM

SnowAngel:	maddie! oh, maaaaddie!
mad maddie:	**yes?**
SnowAngel:	u have to listen to what i'm about to say. now i know ur all excited about your ridiculous speed limit thingie, but u HAVE to change your plans.
mad maddie:	**huh? why?**

Send   Cancel

SnowAngel:	cuz stupid zoe backed out on me. U CAN'T LEAVE ME ALONE WITH DOUG!!!
mad maddie:	**sorry, doll. if i don't go, they won't have enuff drivers.**
SnowAngel:	but this is important!
mad maddie:	**jana's counting on me. she's gonna ride with me and everything. hey, i know—forget doug and come with us!**
SnowAngel:	i can't, that would be cruel. plus, he already invited steve brinks to come 2.
mad maddie:	**u, doug, and steve, hmmm? ooo-la-la.**
SnowAngel:	*stomps foot* this is serious!
mad maddie:	**oh, it is not. invite some other girl to come.**
SnowAngel:	i already tried megan AND kristin AND mary kate, and they're all busy. ur my last chance!!!
mad maddie:	**i hate to be the 1 to break it to u, but ur overreacting as usual. luckily, i have just the thing to cheer u up.**
SnowAngel:	what?
mad maddie:	**it's the "my little pony" quiz! wanna find out which little pony u r?**
SnowAngel:	i'm having a crisis, and u want me to take one of your stupid quizzes?!! no thanks!
mad maddie:	**why, r u scared?**
SnowAngel:	scared of what?
mad maddie:	**scared that my inner dragon might eat your little pony?**
SnowAngel:	omg. u've been waiting to say that, haven't u? u've been, like, really excited to use that line.
mad maddie:	**cuz it's funny. admit it.**
SnowAngel:	u r no help at all.
mad maddie:	**but i'm amusing, which is even better. byeas, angela!**

Send   Cancel

Friday, October 22, 6:00 PM

zoegirl:	hey, angela. this is gonna be quick, cuz mr. h is gonna be here any minute, but i just wanted to give u moral support before your date.
SnowAngel:	it's not a date!!!
zoegirl:	right, right. sorry.
SnowAngel:	change your mind and come with me. please?????
zoegirl:	i can't. i already told u!
SnowAngel:	*pouts*
SnowAngel:	do i have time to tell u what i'm wearing, at least?
zoegirl:	go for it
SnowAngel:	attire: baggy overalls with long-sleeved white t-shirt underneath (NOT tight), doc martens, id bracelet, hair in pathetic attempt at ponytail. oh, and a pair of mom's socks so that mine won't get slimed by the bowling shoe spray.
zoegirl:	baggy overalls and a pathetic ponytail. hmm, r u trying to send a message here?
SnowAngel:	i just don't c any reason to get doug all worked up for nothing.
zoegirl:	how considerate. well, seriously, have fun.
SnowAngel:	i'll try
zoegirl:	bye!

Saturday, October 23, 1:52 PM

mad maddie:	**woo-eee! hey there, angela. ready to hear about my fabulous I-285 adventure?**
SnowAngel:	wait—first i have to tell u something! MY

	PARENTS SAID YES ABOUT CUMBERLAND ISLAND!!!
mad maddie:	**no way! really?**
SnowAngel:	as long as mark and erin will be there to "chaperone" us, they said i could go. *punches the air in wild excitement* i can't believe they actually said yes!
mad maddie:	**angela, that is awesome. we r gonna have so much fun!**
SnowAngel:	i know!!!
SnowAngel:	what about zoe's parents—any word?
mad maddie:	**her mom's gonna call my mom. that's a step, anywayz.**
SnowAngel:	i agree
mad maddie:	**and now, onto my account of our exciting and dramatic speed limit rebellion.**
SnowAngel:	rebellion? i thought u guys were gonna stick to the speed limit exactly. i thought that was the whole point.
mad maddie:	**the point was to rebel AGAINST the speed limit by showing how dumb it is—which we totally did. oh, man, angela, it was wild.**
SnowAngel:	yeah? so tell me.
mad maddie:	**we spread out across I-285 like we planned, each of us in our own lane. then todd spencer gave the thumbs up, which was the signal for everyone to set their speed to 65 mph. so we did. man, u shoulda seen the look on the face of the guy behind us as he realized he wasn't just behind one slow car, he was behind a whole row of slow cars.**
SnowAngel:	was he pissed?
mad maddie:	**majorly. and then it was really funny, cuz slowly the stretch of highway in front of us emptied out, and EVERYONE was stuck behind us.**

SnowAngel: wow

mad maddie: yeah. a couple of ppl honked their horns, and then a couple more, and then everyone was honking and it was the loudest noise i've ever heard. it was cool, but i actually started getting a little freaked out.

SnowAngel: i TOLD u it was dangerous!

mad maddie: i mean, i could FEEL the fury directed at us. it was like a mob was forming or something.

SnowAngel: *shivers*

mad maddie: then cars started passing us in the emergency lane. kaitlin jones was the driver in the far right lane—the one next to the emergency lane—and i was SO glad it wasn't me. this one car whizzed past her, blaring its horn, and then pulled into her lane so closely that he almost cropped her bumper.

SnowAngel: shit, maddie

mad maddie: then someone threw a beer bottle at joe weiss's car. it made this loud crack, like a gun, and i about crapped my pants.

SnowAngel: did it actually HIT joe's car?

mad maddie: no, thank god. by this time cars were passing in the left hand emergency lane 2. this one guy in a volvo pulled right in front of rex and terri and jana and intentionally slammed on his brakes. can u believe that?

SnowAngel: omg, maddie. u guys r sooooooo lucky no one got hurt.

mad maddie: then kaitlin broke out of formation, which meant more cars could get through, and then the rest of us kinda broke apart 2. at first ppl glared and shouted stuff out their windows as they passed, but soon

Send   Cancel

	they must not have recognized us, cuz no one did anything really terrible.
SnowAngel:	u could have been killed, maddie.
mad maddie:	**but i wasn't.**
SnowAngel:	but u COULD have been.
mad maddie:	**the only thing i'm bummed about is that we didn't make it onto the news. think about how great it would have been when they announced it: "cars going the speed limit cause traffic jam"! it would have been hilarious.**
SnowAngel:	hey, wait a sec. that car that slammed on his brakes— did u say he pulled out in front of rex, terri, and jana?
mad maddie:	**what an asshole. it was really scary.**
SnowAngel:	but i thought jana was gonna ride with u.
mad maddie:	**well, she ended up riding with rex and terri instead.**
SnowAngel:	so who rode with u?
mad maddie:	**no one**
SnowAngel:	u were out there with a bunch of maniacs behind u BY YOURSELF?
mad maddie:	**it was no big deal, angela.**
SnowAngel:	was anyone else alone, like kaitlin or joe?
mad maddie:	**what's your point?**
SnowAngel:	they weren't, were they? u were the only one without a passenger.
mad maddie:	**i SAID it was no big deal. ur making it out like . . . i dunno, like jana did some horrible thing by riding with rex instead of me. but i was the one who was there, so i get to choose if it was a problem or not. AND IT WASN'T.**

SnowAngel:	it just doesn't seem very nice, that's all.
mad maddie:	**ur totally reading things into it.**
mad maddie:	**anywayz, unlike some ppl, i'm fine being by myself. i don't need constant reassurance 24-7.**
SnowAngel:	what is that supposed to mean?
mad maddie:	**u figure it out.**
SnowAngel:	u know what, maddie?
SnowAngel:	never mind
mad maddie:	**what? go ahead and say it.**
SnowAngel:	it's just that all our convos seem to end this way these days, and it's getting really annoying. ur always getting huffy over nothing.
mad maddie:	**I'M the one getting huffy?**
SnowAngel:	i'm just saying that i'm glad u had fun with your new friends, even tho none of them actually wanted to be in the same car with u.
SnowAngel:	doesn't that tell u something?
mad maddie:	**it tells me a lot more that U, who's supposedly one of my BEST friends, r so threatened by the fact that i'm hanging out with jana just cuz jana's in such a different social league than u. i'm sorry if ur jealous, angela, but don't take it out on me.**
SnowAngel:	what?!! u r insane if u think i'm jealous of jana whitaker.
mad maddie:	**am i?**
SnowAngel:	okay, whatever. talk to me when ur ready to act like a normal person again!

Send   Cancel

Saturday, October 23, 2:19 PM

SnowAngel:	zoe! aaargh!!!!!!!!
zoegirl:	hey, angela. what's wrong?
SnowAngel:	i just had the most infuriating convo with maddie. grrrr!
zoegirl:	yeah? her name just blipped off my screen. what happened?
SnowAngel:	she was bragging about her 285 adventure—that's what started it. i happened to mention that i didn't think it was very nice that no one rode with her, not even her precious jana, and she totally flipped out and got nasty. god, zoe, it is so weird with her these days! one minute things r fine and dandy, and then the next minute we're at each other's throats!
zoegirl:	things probably just got weird cuz she knows u don't like jana.
SnowAngel:	and she shouldn't either. jana sucks. she's just using maddie for her car—it's so obvious.
zoegirl:	oh, i don't know
SnowAngel:	well, i do
zoegirl:	the whole scene sounded kinda sketchy to me, like a bunch of obnoxious high school kids on a power trip. i'm glad i wasn't there.
SnowAngel:	me 2
zoegirl:	so how about your nite? how'd bowling go?
SnowAngel:	and that's another thing! maddie didn't even bother to ask about that, thank u very much. it's like she thinks my life is 2 boring to talk about.

zoegirl:	well, I'M asking: how was it hanging out with doug and steve? was it fun, or was it miserable?
SnowAngel:	*does wishy-washy thing with hand*
zoegirl:	explain
SnowAngel:	it wasn't soooooo bad. i got chrissy to come with me at the very last minute, and it was actually pretty fun having her along. she kept getting gutter balls, and one time the ball flew off her hand when she was swinging it backward. it bounced across the floor making these big whomping sounds, and we all cracked up.
zoegirl:	chrissy's a great kid
SnowAngel:	yeah. she looked great 2. she wore these faded jeans with embroidery at the bottom, along with a pink t-shirt that said "princess" on it. which sounds dreadful, but on her it looked cute.
zoegirl:	so did doug and steve hit on her? jk
SnowAngel:	*arches one eyebrow* actually . . .
zoegirl:	angela! she's 12!!!
SnowAngel:	they didn't hit on her, exactly.
zoegirl:	what, then?
SnowAngel:	well, like i said, chrissy kept throwing gutter balls, and each time she would laff and get embarrassed and say she was never gonna go bowling again. then one time she went up for her turn, and when she put her fingers in the ball, she stopped and looked confused.
zoegirl:	why?
SnowAngel:	there was a note rolled up in one of the holes! she pulled it out, and it said, "ur doing terrific. don't give up. p.s. i think ur pretty."

Send   Cancel

zoegirl:	awww!
zoegirl:	i take it doug or steve slipped it in there?
SnowAngel:	yes, but for the longest time they didn't admit it. they said it must be from someone at the bowling alley, one of the guys who worked behind the lanes. chrissy's eyes got big, and she blushed like crazy. and then she got even more embarrassed when she rolled a gutter ball again, cuz she was worried that the guy—whoever he was—was watching.
zoegirl:	that totally makes me like doug and steve. what a sweet thing to do.
SnowAngel:	yeah, they kept teasing her about it, saying she had a secret admirer and stuff like that.
SnowAngel:	only . . .
zoegirl:	what?
SnowAngel:	this is really, really, really humiliating, but i actually got kinda jealous. *hides head in shame* this was before i knew doug and steve had planted the note. i kept thinking, "why's that bowling guy flirting with chrissy and not me?"
zoegirl:	silly angela
SnowAngel:	i know. the thought even crossed my mind that the note had been meant for me, and that chrissy had gotten it by accident. how lame, to be jealous of my 12-year-old sister.
zoegirl:	but u were happy for her 2, so that's ok. and doug and steve probably wanted to slip notes in your bowling ball, but they knew they couldn't, cuz that would be, like, 2 real.

Send   Cancel

SnowAngel:	*big mushy hug* thanks, zo. u always make me feel better.
SnowAngel:	so what about u? how was your bingo date with mr. h?
zoegirl:	my wild nite at the nursing home? jk. it was nice. really nice. i helped all these old ppl with their cards, and it made me feel all floaty inside.
SnowAngel:	floaty?
zoegirl:	u know, like when u c a sunset, or when ur outside looking at the stars? that huge, happy feeling like ur connected to all the good things in the world.
SnowAngel:	wow. that's awesome.
zoegirl:	it made me wanna do more stuff like that, stuff that doesn't involve school and grades and all that pressure. they have a volunteer program, and i'm thinking about signing up.
SnowAngel:	but what about mr. h—did anything happen with him?
zoegirl:	well . . . u have to promise not to tell anyone, ok? not even maddie. (and unlike maddie, i honestly mean it.)
SnowAngel:	i promise, i promise! did he kiss u?!! 😲
zoegirl:	no, no, no, nothing like that. but—and i'm probably wrong, and i know i'll sound really arrogant for even saying this—but i'm starting to think that maybe there could be something b/w us, something more than the fact that he's my teacher.
SnowAngel:	what do u mean?
zoegirl:	i think maybe he . . . u know. likes me.
SnowAngel:	well, duh, zoe. u don't c mr. miklos schmoozing me for bingo dates, now do u? *shudders* ew, what a horrible image.

zoegirl:	u don't think i'm being ridiculous? u think there's, like, a chance?
SnowAngel:	do u WANT there to be a chance?
zoegirl:	i don't know. maybe? oh, wow, i'm turning bright red just saying it out loud—and i'm NOT even saying out loud, i'm typing it over the computer. thank god we're not talking in person. i'd probably faint.
SnowAngel:	whoa. this is so . . . lifetime-channel-ish.
zoegirl:	gee, thanks
SnowAngel:	no, it's just that u expect things like this to happen in movies, not in real life. only it IS happening in real life.
zoegirl:	kinda scary, huh?
SnowAngel:	i guess i thought it was just a game, something we talked about just for fun. but ur seriously falling for him, aren't u?
zoegirl:	i don't know. i think about him a lot. more than a lot. and last nite, when he dropped me off . . .
SnowAngel:	yes?
zoegirl:	we were sitting in his car, talking, and he reached over and brushed my hair off my face. i know that sounds like nothing, but the way he did it made it seem like more.
SnowAngel:	like how?
zoegirl:	just really gentle, like it meant something to be touching me.
SnowAngel:	wow
zoegirl:	then he pulled back his hand and said, "ur in 10th grade, zoe." and i said, "i know." then he said, "ur 15," and i said, "i know."

ttyl

SnowAngel:	oh, man. he was totally, like, admitting he was into u.
zoegirl:	then he pushed back my hair again, tucking it behind my ear, and . . . i don't know. it's the way he looked at me, like he was saying 2 different things at the same time.
zoegirl:	it sounds really stupid, doesn't it?
SnowAngel:	it doesn't sound stupid, zo. it sounds . . . big.
zoegirl:	yeah. that's kinda how it feels 2.
SnowAngel:	i'm excited for u, since u like him back and everything. but r u sure this is ok? i mean, he's a TEACHER, zoe.
zoegirl:	i know. and probably nothing more will happen, not til i graduate anyway. which is only 2 years away.
SnowAngel:	true
zoegirl:	hey, i'm gonna get off now. ttyl?
SnowAngel:	yeah, call me this afternoon. maybe we can go get ice cream or something.
zoegirl:	sounds good!

Monday, October 25, 7:17 PM

mad maddie:	**hey, zo-ster**
zoegirl:	hey, mads. i saw u drive by my house this afternoon— why didn't u stop?
mad maddie:	**i couldn't, cuz i was already running late. i honked, tho.**
zoegirl:	yeah, i heard. what were u late for?
mad maddie:	**i had a doctor's appointment. it was my annual physical.**
zoegirl:	and?
mad maddie:	**no shots, baby!**
zoegirl:	wh-hoo!

138

Send   Cancel

mad maddie:	at the end, the doc got all serious and asked me a bunch of questions. doc: "r u sexually active?" me: "sadly, no." doc: "do u ever drink?" me: "ummm . . . " doc: "have u ever thought of killing yourself?" me: "maybe. doesn't everyone?"
zoegirl:	good one
mad maddie:	doc: "yes, well, have u ever made a plan?" me: "no, unless continuing to sit through geometry counts as a plan." doc: "excuse me?" me: "meet mr. miklos and u'll understand. u'll die of boredom."
zoegirl:	u did not really say that.
mad maddie:	maybe i did, maybe i didn't. i am a woman of mystery.
zoegirl:	speaking of mystery, u have to tell me about u and ian! u started to tell me in homeroom, and then stupid ms. andrist got all busy with announcements.
mad maddie:	our saturday nite snuggle-fest, u mean?
zoegirl:	has he kissed u yet—a real kiss?
mad maddie:	he STILL hasn't! he's, like, the snuggle king, which is nice, but i'm ready for more. i keep telling myself that i should make the move myself, but i keep chickening out.
zoegirl:	he's probably nervous 2
mad maddie:	i guess. on saturday, we ended the nite with a hug.
zoegirl:	awww!
mad maddie:	awww, yourself. i'm a growing girl. i have needs, dammit!
zoegirl:	he'll get there, just give him time.
mad maddie:	or put on crotchless panties and do a lap dance for him.
zoegirl:	there is that

mad maddie:	**i know that makes me sound like a slut—and i really don't mean it like that. and i'm not pulling an angela, either, like "ooo, he's THE ONE." it's just that ian's awesome, and i want things to get deeper, u know? and if things got more physical, maybe that would happen.**
zoegirl:	i know what u mean
mad maddie:	**u do?**
zoegirl:	i'm not a saint, maddie
mad maddie:	**well . . . it's different, tho.**
zoegirl:	how?
mad maddie:	**cuz with mr. h, u know it'll never go further than a crush, which is totally not the same thing.**
mad maddie:	**anyway, i'm outta here. the moms has the meatloaf on the table, and it's calling my name. l8rs!**

Tuesday, October 26, 7:30 PM

mad maddie:	**hey, angela. u just get home?**
SnowAngel:	yeah, how'd u know?
mad maddie:	**i called your home line a few minutes ago, but chrissy said u were at drama club. how's the schlanker?**
SnowAngel:	BEN is superb, thanks for asking. he told me a funny story about something that happened at starbucks. wanna hear?
mad maddie:	**the schlank-master goes to starbucks? i'd figure him for aurora or churchill grounds, one of those coffee joints where he could snap his fingers and wear a black beret.**
SnowAngel:	*narrows eyes* do not make fun of the schlank-master—i mean BEN!!! do u wanna hear the story or not?

Send   Cancel

mad maddie:	**press on, by all means.**
SnowAngel:	well, he was sitting in starbucks reading the newspaper when this frat boy came up and asked if he could look at the sports section. ben handed it to him and said, "sure, i don't read that section anyway." then the frat boy snorted and said, "yeah, i kinda figured."
mad maddie:	**asshole**
SnowAngel:	so ben stood up, took the paper out of the guy's hands, and said, "your reading privileges have been revoked. sorry!"
mad maddie:	**ha! that's awesome**
SnowAngel:	i know. he is my hero.
mad maddie:	**tits, man**
SnowAngel:	please
SnowAngel:	hey, do u know what i just realized on the way home from school? HALLOWEEN IS LESS THAN A WEEK AWAY! what r we gonna do this year? r we gonna go trick-or-treating?
mad maddie:	**hell, yeah. free candy!**
SnowAngel:	u don't think we're 2 old?
mad maddie:	**let's try this again: FREE CANDY!!!**
SnowAngel:	well, what should we go as?
mad maddie:	**let me think about it. do u care if i invite ian?**
SnowAngel:	sure, if u think he'd wanna come. he has to come up with his own costume, tho. he can't glom onto us.
mad maddie:	**i'll swing the idea by him and c what he says. byeas!**

Send   Cancel

141

Tuesday, October 26, 7:46 PM

SnowAngel:	yay! i just had a convo with maddie and it was NORMAL!!!
zoegirl:	wh-hoo!
SnowAngel:	i know. i've been like trying really hard to be cool around her, but at school it's impossible cuz she's always tagging after jana. *barf* but our IM chat just now was totally fine. i'm so glad! ☺
zoegirl:	me 2. that's awesome.
SnowAngel:	and now off to watch "gilmore girls." bye!

Wednesday, October 27, 5:33 PM

zoegirl:	hey, mads. guess what?!!
mad maddie:	**what?**
zoegirl:	MOM AND DAD SAID I CAN GO TO CUMBERLAND ISLAND!!!
mad maddie:	**r u yanking my chain?**
zoegirl:	no, they really did! i almost had them sign a piece of paper swearing they wouldn't change their minds, but i thought that might be pushing it.
mad maddie:	**zoe, that's awesome!!!**
mad maddie:	**how did this happen?!!**
zoegirl:	well, remember in homeroom how i told u my mom thought i needed to spend my break doing something more productive?
mad maddie:	**your mom is such a type A**
zoegirl:	yeah, cuz she has to be. that's how she gets everything done.

Send   Cancel

zoegirl:	anyway, i thought about it all day, how i could make the trip "productive," and when i got home from school i called a park ranger. 1st i talked to him and then i gave the phone to mom, and he must have been ultra-convincing, cuz now mom's all fired up about my going on an "environmentalist" adventure. she thinks i'll be able to use it in my college essays.
mad maddie:	**oh lord. do they know i'm bringing my mini-tv?**
zoegirl:	i left that part out, as well as the part about the collapsible chaise lounges. but the point is I CAN GO!!!
mad maddie:	**wh-hoo! cumberland island, here we come!**
zoegirl:	in like 4 weeks!
mad maddie:	**which means we have to kick into maximum planning mode, like what kinda food to bring and stuff like that. and we'll have to get our camping gear ready. u DO have a sleeping bag, right?**
zoegirl:	i do
mad maddie:	**a real one, not one with the little mermaid on it?**
zoegirl:	a real one, don't worry.
mad maddie:	**good, cuz angela's already borrowing my dad's.**
zoegirl:	ha
mad maddie:	**hey—i found a great website for u. it's called jesus.com.**
zoegirl:	maddie . . .
mad maddie:	**i'm not kidding. i feel bad that i've teased u so much, so i've started doing my own religious exploration.**
zoegirl:	uhhuh, right
mad maddie:	**i'm serious, swear to god. just check it out, ok?**
zoegirl:	i don't believe u

zoegirl:	r u TRULY serious? for real?
mad maddie:	**cross my heart and hope to die.**
zoegirl:	well . . . thanks. that's really cool of u.
mad maddie:	**ain't it the truth. byeas!**

Wednesday, October 27, 5:51 PM

zoegirl:	maddie, get your on-line butt over here this instant!
mad maddie:	**zoe! quel surprise!**
zoegirl:	*Young women interested in bathing with Jesus can now have their dream come true?!!*
mad maddie:	**hee, hee**
zoegirl:	*Shower can be exchanged for bubble bath upon request?!!!*
mad maddie:	**oh, i'd go for the bubble bath. definitely more romantic.**
zoegirl:	u sent me to a porn site!!! WHY did i believe for a second that u were serious?
mad maddie:	**i have no idea**
mad maddie:	**but it's not a porn site. it's a dating service. don't tell me u'd turn down a date with jesus.**
zoegirl:	that guy is not jesus! that guy is a psycho!!!
mad maddie:	**so u didn't take the compatibility quiz?**
zoegirl:	omg, did U?
mad maddie:	**u bet your bootie. it said, *You scored in the lowest tenth percentile. You probably don't know what kind of woman Jesus is looking for.***
zoegirl:	well, that's true.
mad maddie:	**i took it for u 2, since i knew u wouldn't. wanna hear your results?**

Send   Cancel

zoegirl:	what do u mean, u took it for me? u didn't give him my name, did u?
mad maddie:	**here r your results: *You scored above average. Hopefully you don't live too far away. When you contact Jesus, please mention that you are quiz taker #1026747910-29730.***
zoegirl:	oh. my. god.
mad maddie:	**that's the spirit!**
zoegirl:	i don't believe u, maddie.
mad maddie:	**did u c the part about how he gets to take a picture of u in the bubble bath and post it on his website? IF u go out with him, that is.**
zoegirl:	shit
zoegirl:	he's gonna track us both down and murder us.
mad maddie:	**or at least wash our feet. i told jana about the site, and she thought it was hilarious.**
zoegirl:	wait a minute—u guys IM?
mad maddie:	**i IM lots of ppl, zoe**
mad maddie:	**jana especially liked the endorsements section, where he gives his lubricant rec in 12 tasty flavors.**
zoegirl:	yes, well, that's enuff fun and games for me for today.
mad maddie:	**ur not gonna contact jesus, then? this is a once in a lifetime opportunity!**
zoegirl:	bye, maddie!
mad maddie:	**hallelujah, praise god!**

Thursday, October 28, 9:02 PM

SnowAngel:	hola, maddie. u said u had an idea for our halloween costumes?

mad maddie:	yeah, how about we go as fungus, mold, and dust?
SnowAngel:	*wrinkles nose*
mad maddie:	c'mon, it would be great. we could get some cotton batting and spray paint it a nasty green color, then glue it on garbage bags or something.
SnowAngel:	☺
mad maddie:	do u have a better plan? u've trashed all my other suggestions.
SnowAngel:	and u've trashed mine. i still think the three little pigs would be adorable.
mad maddie:	yeah, only i don't do adorable. so what do u say— fungus, mold, and dust?
SnowAngel:	hmm. if i was dust, i could be a dust bunny. that could be cute.
mad maddie:	i wanna be fungus, so i can say "there's a fungus among us."
SnowAngel:	i'm NOT gonna look all gross, tho. i'll wear a gray leotard and pin on a fluffy tail, and i'll glue some ears to a headband.
mad maddie:	snazz yourself up however u want. i'll be the one in a garbage bag.
SnowAngel:	then it's settled. i'll call zoe and tell her she's mold.
mad maddie:	groovy. byeas!

Saturday, October 30, 11:35 AM

mad maddie:	hey, angela. tell me the truth: do i have a "mean" look?
SnowAngel:	what, other than your regular expression?
mad maddie:	ha ha

Send   Cancel

mad maddie:	**wait—r u serious?**
SnowAngel:	first tell me what ur talking about. who said u have a mean look?
mad maddie:	**my cousin lily. she came over for dinner last nite with her parents, and she said i gave her a mean look. she'd said something about wanting to be a hairdresser when she gets older, and in my mind i rolled my eyes. BUT THAT'S ALL.**
SnowAngel:	what's so bad about wanting to be a hairdresser?
mad maddie:	**nothing, i guess. it's just such a girlie thing to wanna be. i want lily to grow up tough and fiesty.**
SnowAngel:	like u?
mad maddie:	**she's only 10—she shouldn't dream of doing ppl's hair. anywayz, she said i give mean looks all the time. do i?!!**
SnowAngel:	*ponders*
mad maddie:	**u have to THINK about it?**
SnowAngel:	well, u do have this disdainful air about u sometimes, like everyone's really dumb except u. and u have this way of cutting your eyes at someone that can make her kinda shrivel up.
SnowAngel:	it's not a BAD thing, necessarily.
mad maddie:	**oh god**
SnowAngel:	u've given it to me a couple of times, your mean look.
mad maddie:	**like when?**
SnowAngel:	like today during our free period when i happened to mention to jana that u have a boyfriend.
mad maddie:	**i did not**
SnowAngel:	u made me wanna crawl up and die.

ttyl

mad maddie:	but that's cuz ian's not technically my "boyfriend." it sounds so so teeny-bopper-ish when u put it like that.
SnowAngel:	whatever.
SnowAngel:	hey, do I have a mean look?
mad maddie:	u?!!
SnowAngel:	yes, me. is that so impossible?
mad maddie:	u do not have a mean look, angela. sorry to disappoint u.
SnowAngel:	oh, what do u know. i bet i DO have a mean look. i bet it makes ppl quake in their boots.
mad maddie:	if by "ppl" u mean "little baby kittens," maybe. before they wobble over and lick your face.
SnowAngel:	*shoots daggers with eyes*
mad maddie:	aw, look at all the baby kittens coming over! they're so sweet!
SnowAngel:	screw u
SnowAngel:	so r we still on for tomorrow nite?
mad maddie:	i told ian we'd meet at 7:00 at zoe's house, since she lives in the ritziest neighborhood. we're talking full-size snickers, baby. none of that "fun size" malarkey for OUR healthy appetites.
SnowAngel:	right on. ttyl!

Sunday, October 31, 5:45 PM

SnowAngel:	BOO!
zoegirl:	hey, angela. boo to u 2.
SnowAngel:	got your costume all ready for tonite?
zoegirl:	pretty much. u?
SnowAngel:	yep. i ended up making my bunny fur out of dryer lint

148

	(since i'm a DUST bunny, get it?), which i glued strategically over my leotard. *wiggles fanny suggestively*
zoegirl:	omg, only u would find a way to sex up a dust bunny.
SnowAngel:	me, to gorgeous trick-or-treater: "hey there, big boy. want me to nibble your carrot?"
zoegirl:	me, to gorgeous trick-or-treater: "hey there, big boy. want me to give u jock itch?"
SnowAngel:	"mold" doesn't offer as many opportunities for seduction, that's true. perhaps if u offered to itch his jock . . .
zoegirl:	i'll pass, thanks
SnowAngel:	hey, doug called about an hour ago, and i kinda invited him to come with us. steve 2. do u care?
zoegirl:	is doug your gorgeous trick-or-treater?
SnowAngel:	NO! god, no. it's just that he asked if i wanted to go to a party with him, and i turned him down since i already had plans with y'all. so then i asked him if HE wanted to join US, totally expecting him to decline. only he didn't.
zoegirl:	i'm just teasing u, angela. i don't care if they come.
SnowAngel:	they're, uh, dressing up as star trek characters.
zoegirl:	why does that not surprise me?
SnowAngel:	maddie better not make fun of them. i tried calling to warn her, but no one answered.
zoegirl:	if she gets here before u do, i'll tell her. but she'll be fine with it. c u in an hour?
SnowAngel:	*winks and smarmily points finger* u got it, hotshot. c ya!

Monday, November 1, 1:05 AM

mad maddie: angela? u awake?

SnowAngel: wtf, maddie? it's one in the morning! WHERE THE HELL WERE U LAST NITE?!!

mad maddie: thank god ur awake. thank god ur on-line.

SnowAngel: yeah, cuz i've been sitting here watching for your name on my buddy list, which believe me has NOT been fun. i called your house 3 different times, but no one ever answered. i was afraid u'd gotten into an accident or something!

mad maddie: relax, ok? god, i can hardly keep my ffinre on the keys.

SnowAngel: your what?

mad maddie: my fingers. that's what i mean

mad maddie: god, they're fat

SnowAngel: your fingers? what r u talking about?

mad maddie: i hate myself. i know u do 2. eveyroen does, so u can just admit it.

SnowAngel: maddie, what is going on? ur acting REALLY weird.

mad maddie: well, u would be 2 if u were me. whihc u should be glad ur not, and i'm so not kidding.

mad maddie: anyeay, it's not my fault. someone said it was spiekd with everclear. whatever it was, it was nasty, like nasty red kool-aid.

SnowAngel: omg. r u DRUNK?

mad maddie: i had 3 galsess. it was nasty.

SnowAngel: oh, this is just great. where the hell were u that u were drinking everclear punch? and why was that so much more important than hanging out with us like

150

u'd promised? I showed up, zoe showed up, doug and steve showed up, even *IAN* showed up. where the hell were u?

mad maddie: stop. don't be mean to me, ok?

mad maddie: sonething bad happened, angela. really bad.

SnowAngel: what do u mean?

SnowAngel: shit. WERE u in an accident?

mad maddie: i went to this party with jana. it was at her brother's frat house.

SnowAngel: WHAT?!! U BLEW US OFF FOR JANA?!!

mad maddie: and there was this punch, and jana was being really funny and mkating me drink it, but really i think she was mad at me cuz

mad maddie: never mind

SnowAngel: cuz what?

mad maddie: cuz of something i said which was toally a joke, but she got mad anyway. and then i must have really been out of it cuz i ended dancing on this table and jana was laffing and i wsa laffing only now i don't think it was so hilarius. cuz, angela?

SnowAngel: what happened, mads?

mad maddie: my shirt says "x-men 2, the time has come."

SnowAngel: u don't have an x-men shirt

SnowAngel: u wouldn't be caught dead in an x-men shirt.

mad maddie: i know

SnowAngel: so where's YOUR shirt?

mad maddie: gone, i guess, cuz i'm sure as hell not going back to the frat house to get it.

Send   Cancel

151

SnowAngel:	your shirt is at the frat house?
mad maddie:	**same goes for my bra. adios! sayonara!**
SnowAngel:	wait a minute. are u saying what i think ur saying? did u, like, take your shirt off on purpose? AND your bra?
mad maddie:	**ppl threw money at me, angela. i remember ppl thwoing, like, dimes and quarters and shit.**
SnowAngel:	holy fuck
SnowAngel:	and where was jana during all of this? why didn't she do something to stop it?
mad maddie:	**gee, i dunno, cuz i was embarraasing the hell out of her? she must HATE me now.**
SnowAngel:	but why didn't she just pull u away? or get u to go to the bathroom with her or something?
mad maddie:	**she was drunk 2. it wasn't her fault.**
SnowAngel:	u sure? cuz i'm thinking about what u said, about how she was mad at u. and i'm thinking that it sounds incredibly unlikely that she was just, like, an innocent bystander in all this.
mad maddie:	**wtf?!!!**
mad maddie:	**i don't even know what ur tyring to say. my head is pounding, i feel like shit, and i just wanna go to bed.**
mad maddie:	**i thought talking to u would make me feel bettre, but it's just mkaing me feel worse.**
SnowAngel:	maddie, hold on. i'm sorry for being snotty, it's just that the whole situation sounds really strange.
mad maddie:	**AND DON'T TELL ZOE. god, that's the last thing i need, having her get all holy on me.**
SnowAngel:	she wouldn't do that.

mad maddie:	**don't tell. i mean it.**
SnowAngel:	i won't, i won't. but r u gonna be ok?
SnowAngel:	and what about your parents?!! did they freak when u came in?
mad maddie:	**they're at some paarty, and mark's at erin's. i'm all alone.**
SnowAngel:	at least u didn't get busted. THAT'S good.
mad maddie:	**whoopee**
SnowAngel:	ur worrying me, maddie. do u want me to come over?
mad maddie:	**and how would u do that?**
SnowAngel:	i dunno. i'd find a way.
mad maddie:	**no thanks**
SnowAngel:	r u SURE?
mad maddie:	**i'm positive. i just wannt go to bed.**
SnowAngel:	all right. well, we'll talk more tomorrow.
mad maddie:	**whatevs**
SnowAngel:	*hug hug hug* good nite! i luv u! EVERYTHING'S GONNA BE OK!!!

Monday, November 1, 6:21 PM

zoegirl:	maddie, good. ur home.
mad maddie:	**if ur IMing just to yell at me some more, i don't wanna hear it.**
zoegirl:	what? i never yelled at u.
mad maddie:	**in homeroom u did. maybe u didn't yell, but close enuff.**
zoegirl:	well, i'm still mad that u blew us off, but i'm worried about u 2. u seemed so down today.
mad maddie:	**whatevs**

Send   Cancel

153

zoegirl:	is something else going on? something other than the fact that u went to that stupid frat party?
mad maddie:	**there's nothing going on. god.**
zoegirl:	then why r u acting this way?
zoegirl:	if anyone has the right to be upset, it's me and angela, not u.
mad maddie:	**oh, now that's supportive. if something HAD happened, i'd really wanna tell u now.**
zoegirl:	so something DID happen! i saw u talking to jana at lunch, and she didn't look happy. did u 2 have a fight?
mad maddie:	**what do u mean she didn't look happy?**
zoegirl:	u know, like she wasn't into being there. like how she kept glancing around, as if she was really bored.
mad maddie:	**she was distracted. she had to find terri to get the english assignment.**
zoegirl:	if u say so
mad maddie:	**ppl do get distracted, zoe. not everybody is into every conversation every second of her life.**
zoegirl:	ok, fine
mad maddie:	**u act like u don't believe me. why? is there something ur not telling me?**
zoegirl:	hey, i've told u everything i know, which is nothing. is there something UR not telling ME? u told me about going to her brother's party, but i get the sense maybe there's more. is there?
zoegirl:	???
mad maddie:	**i don't want u flipping out.**
zoegirl:	i'm your FRIEND. just tell me.

Send   Cancel

mad maddie:	**maybe we r having a fight, me and jana. i dunno. it's all so screwed up.**
zoegirl:	did she do something?
mad maddie:	**u said u weren't gonna flip out!**
zoegirl:	what, i can't even ask questions?
mad maddie:	**this is exactly why i didn't wanna talk to u!**
zoegirl:	just tell me what's going on!!!
mad maddie:	**fine. yes, jana's pissed at me, which i totally don't get. i had a few cups of punch, that's all. anywayz, so did she.**
zoegirl:	did u get drunk? as in, DRUNK drunk?
zoegirl:	i thought u knew better than that.
mad maddie:	**oh, that's great. what r u saying, like father like daughter?**
zoegirl:	NO! i didn't mean it like that, i swear. i don't even know what i was talking about.
zoegirl:	but is that why jana got mad?
mad maddie:	**no**
zoegirl:	then WHY?
mad maddie:	**cuz according to her, i made her look bad.**
zoegirl:	what?! how?
mad maddie:	**she said i was out of control and that i made a complete fool out of myself. but SHE was the one egging me on the whole time! anywayz, i don't think it's really about that.**
zoegirl:	egging u on to do what, drink the punch?
mad maddie:	**i think it's about something i said earlier that afternoon.**
zoegirl:	yes?
mad maddie:	**c, she'd called and asked if i could give her a ride to her brother's frat house, and i'd said sure. so i drove over and**

	picked her up, and as we were driving to georgia tech, she told me this really funny story about terri.
zoegirl:	what was the story?
mad maddie:	well, terri has this thing about other ppl's spit, right? and she never wants to share her food or her water bottle or anything. she's totally anal about it. so at lunch on friday, when terri got up to get a napkin, jana took terri's fork and licked it. then everyone else at the table licked it, 2. jana waited til terri came back and started eating, and then she told her what they'd done. isn't that hysterical?
zoegirl:	no, it's disgusting. what did terri do?
mad maddie:	she freaked, obviously. and she must have really cussed jana out, cuz in the car jana was talking about what a bitch terri was for getting so bent out of shape. and i was like, "oh, like u wouldn't? what about when margaret called u a lesbo?"
zoegirl:	margaret called jana a lesbo?
mad maddie:	i wasn't there, but apparently it was after PE one day last week. jana was strutting around in the locker room, i guess she was naked, and margaret asked if she was a lesbian. supposedly she did it in this super concerned way, like, "it's ok, u can tell US," and it made everyone crack up.
zoegirl:	lovely
mad maddie:	but when i brought it up in the car , i was completely joking. i was just teasing her, like how u and me and angela do with each other.
zoegirl:	so what did jana say?

Send   Cancel

mad maddie: her face got hard and she said, "oh, sweet, coming from u. ur the biggest lesbo around, always staring at me and laffing at everything i say."

zoegirl: ouch

mad maddie: i know. i was like, SHIT.

mad maddie: so i totally backed off, and time passed and i thought everything was ok. i mean, i went inside with her when we got to her brother's frat house, and it seemed like things were fine b/w us. she kept introducing me to ppl and getting me to help pick out cds and stuff.

zoegirl: did u just forget that u were supposed to be meeting us?

mad maddie: no! at eight i was like, "i have GOT to go," and jana was like, "stay," and i was afraid she'd get pissed again if i didn't. and then she said, "your friends have probably left by now anyway."

zoegirl: we hadn't. we waited until 8:30.

mad maddie: i SAID i was sorry. anywayz, the party didn't even turn out to be fun, so u can be happy about that. in fact, it was worse than un-fun.

zoegirl: what do u mean?

mad maddie: god. i just wish jana would start acting normal again, cuz she, like, wouldn't even talk to me in study hall. is it really over that stupid lesbo remark?

zoegirl: jana's a bitch, maddie. and u know i don't use that word.

mad maddie: whatevs

mad maddie: so . . . angela said ian showed up at your house. was he mad?

zoegirl: that u weren't there? more like hurt, i'd say.

mad maddie:	**shit**
zoegirl:	he kept
zoegirl:	never mind
mad maddie:	**what?**
zoegirl:	he kept asking questions, like "do u think she's ok? do u think she got lost?" like there's any way u could get lost driving to my house.
mad maddie:	**shit**
zoegirl:	don't worry. u can call and straighten things out.
mad maddie:	**no thanks, i'll just wait til i c him. i don't think i can handle another guilt trip right now.**
mad maddie:	**god, this sucks**
zoegirl:	look, maddie. it's over. ian will understand when u explain what happened. as for jana, i know ur upset, but maybe it's for the best. maybe it just goes to show what kind of friend she really is.
mad maddie:	**could she really hate me so much that she wouldn't want to be my friend anymore?**
mad maddie:	**no. she'll come around.**
mad maddie:	**anywayz, DON'T tell angela any of what i told u. i don't want the 2 of u talking about this behind my back.**
zoegirl:	maddie! we would never do that.
mad maddie:	**still, i want u to promise.**
zoegirl:	i promise, i promise
mad maddie:	**cuz like u said, it's over. and now i'm gonna go crash, maybe take a nap.**
zoegirl:	be easy on yourself! bye!

Send   Cancel

lauren myracle

SnowAngel:	hey, zo
zoegirl:	hey, angela. have fun at the mall?
SnowAngel:	ehh, it was ok. i kept worrying about maddie, tho.
zoegirl:	u 2, huh?
SnowAngel:	i called her from the gap and told her the pastel sweater sets were on sale, and she didn't even snort.
zoegirl:	ooo, that's bad
SnowAngel:	did she happen to tell u anything about what happened? u know, at that frat party?
zoegirl:	uh, not really. just that she didn't have fun. did she tell u anything, when u talked to her on the phone?
SnowAngel:	the same, really
zoegirl:	huh. well, she'll snap out of it. she'll be ok.
SnowAngel:	i guess. only . . . i kinda think there's more going on than maybe she's admitting.
zoegirl:	what do u mean?
SnowAngel:	well, u didn't hear it from me, but i think something happened b/w her and jana.
zoegirl:	so she DID tell u!
SnowAngel:	tell me what?
zoegirl:	about how maddie called jana a lesbo, but only cuz margaret called her that first.
SnowAngel:	wtf?
zoegirl:	the big fight they had—isn't that what ur talking about? and how maddie got wasted and made a complete fool out of herself?

SnowAngel:	omg, she told me not to tell u!
zoegirl:	she told me not to tell u!
SnowAngel:	that is sooooo maddie. i can't believe this!
SnowAngel:	except i hadn't heard about the lesbo remark, which kinda throws a new spin on things.
zoegirl:	it does?
SnowAngel:	well, yeah. i'm talking about the whole shirt thing. cuz if jana wanted to get back at maddie, u'd think she'd do something that didn't involve, like, a girl doing a striptease. cuz what does THAT say about jana, u know?
zoegirl:	HUH?
SnowAngel:	don't make me say it. it's 2 embarrassing. and for everyone to be throwing money? i know maddie was drunk, and i'm not BLAMING her, but god.
zoegirl:	angela, what the hell r u talking about?
SnowAngel:	r u being serious? u said she told u!
zoegirl:	i'm beginning to think she left some parts out.
SnowAngel:	*gulps* uh . . .
zoegirl:	u have to tell me, angela. u started it, and u have to finish it. WHAT HAPPENED?
SnowAngel:	shit
SnowAngel:	well, maddie got drunk on kool-aid punch, right? and she didn't exactly explain it, but i get the sense that jana got her to do, like, a table dance in front of the whole party.
zoegirl:	no way. that's impossible.
SnowAngel:	she ended up with somebody else's shirt on, zo. and no bra.

Send   Cancel

zoegirl:	oh god. all she told me was that she'd gotten a little out of control.
SnowAngel:	that's one way to put it, i guess.
zoegirl:	SHIT, angela
SnowAngel:	i know
zoegirl:	this is terrible. i can't even get my head around it.
SnowAngel:	but listen, we've got to be super careful not to let on that we talked. she'd flip if she knew.
zoegirl:	uh, YEAH. i think we should pretty much not bring the party up at all, but if SHE wants to talk about it, she can.
SnowAngel:	mainly we'll just act normal, altho we'll be extra extra nice to her.
zoegirl:	sounds good
zoegirl:	still, angela. god.
SnowAngel:	yep
zoegirl:	all right. well, bye!

Monday, November 1, 8:21 PM

SnowAngel:	it's strange, isn't it, that maddie hates her dad's drinking so much, and then she goes out and does the same thing?
zoegirl:	i know. i thought of that 2.
SnowAngel:	poor maddie!!!

Tuesday, November 2, 9:30 PM

zoegirl:	hey there, mads
mad maddie:	**hey, zo. wazzup?**
zoegirl:	nothing, just killing time before bed.

Send   Cancel

161

mad maddie:	**yeah, me 2**
zoegirl:	wanna hear something gross?
mad maddie:	**i guess**
zoegirl:	i ran into megan at eckerd's, and she was buying one of those long wrap-around bandages for her 2-year-old brother. he fell off a chair or something, only the chair fell with him, and it landed on his hands and peeled 3 of his fingernails off. isn't that awful?
mad maddie:	**oh, ick**
zoegirl:	i know. they have to keep his hand wrapped up for like a week, which is why megan was buying more bandages. she said his fingers look all sad and raw, like little sea creatures without their shells.
mad maddie:	**poor kid. that sucks.**
zoegirl:	yeah
zoegirl:	that's all i IMed to say, really. i just wanted to shoot the breeze.
mad maddie:	**shoot away**
zoegirl:	i already did
mad maddie:	**oh**
zoegirl:	so . . . i guess i'll go to bed.
zoegirl:	unless u have anything u wanna talk about?
mad maddie:	**nope, not really**
zoegirl:	that's ok. ur doing all right, tho?
mad maddie:	**hmm. jana's still acting as if i no longer exist, terri and margaret whisper to each other every time they c me, and i still haven't gotten up the nerve to call ian. let's c, is that all?**

Send   Cancel

mad maddie:	**oh, and u and angela r walking on eggshells around me cuz u think i'm gonna collapse. so yes, i'm absolutely fabulous. thanks for asking.**
zoegirl:	i'm sorry. i didn't mean to make things worse.
mad maddie:	**and DON'T say "at least u didn't have your fingernails pulled off," cuz i so don't wanna hear it.**
zoegirl:	well, is there anything i can do?
mad maddie:	**yeah, go to bed and stop fussing over me. it makes me feel pathetic.**
zoegirl:	ur not pathetic, maddie.
mad maddie:	**whatevs. nite, zo.**
zoegirl:	uh, ok. good nite.

Wednesday, November 3, 8:21 PM

SnowAngel:	mad-a-lad-a-ding-dong!
mad maddie:	**ouch. let's tone down the enthusiasm, shall we?**
SnowAngel:	wazzup? where'd u disappear to after math?
mad maddie:	**nowhere, i just went home.**
SnowAngel:	but i thought we were going out for ice cream!
mad maddie:	**u had a drama club meeting, remember?**
SnowAngel:	u could have waited. it only lasted an hour.
mad maddie:	**i felt like going home, that's all.**
SnowAngel:	well, let's go now. *bats eyelashes adorably*
mad maddie:	**no thanks**
SnowAngel:	why not?
mad maddie:	**i'm not in the mood.**
SnowAngel:	how can u not be in the mood for ice cream? c'mon, sling yourself into the gremlin and come pick me up.

Send   Cancel

163

mad maddie:	**sorry**
SnowAngel:	pralines 'n 'cream, mint chocolate chip, chocolate mousse . . .
mad maddie:	**i said no, angela. give it up.**
SnowAngel:	u can't stay holed up 4ever, u know.
mad maddie:	**oh god, here it comes**
SnowAngel:	well, it's true. u've got to show jana that u could care less what she thinks of u. she can rotate thru whatever friends she wants to, and they can call each other "lesbos" all day long if that's what gets them off. but ur sticking with us, baby.
mad maddie:	**that's a great plan. only i DO care what jana thinks of me.**
SnowAngel:	but why?
mad maddie:	**wait a minute. who told u about margaret calling jana a lesbo?**
SnowAngel:	u did
mad maddie:	**no, i didn't**
SnowAngel:	obviously u did, or how would i know?
mad maddie:	**fuck**
mad maddie:	**did u talk to zoe? don't lie!**
SnowAngel:	what r u talking about? of course i talked to zoe. i talk to zoe every day.
mad maddie:	**u know what i mean. did u talk to zoe about . . . that nite?**
SnowAngel:	no!
mad maddie:	**did u?**
SnowAngel:	NO, i swear!
mad maddie:	**ANGELA!**

SnowAngel:	if i tell u, will u promise not to be mad?
mad maddie:	**omg! i can't believe u!**
mad maddie:	**PLEASE tell me u didn't tell her about the x-men shirt. PLEASE.**
SnowAngel:	she said u'd told her! i thought she already knew! anyway, it's your fault for telling us each a little bit and then expecting us not to worry about u!
mad maddie:	**i hate u, angela. i really do.**
SnowAngel:	don't say that. it was totally an accident, ok? i'm sorry!!!
mad maddie:	**FUCK. did u tell her everything?**
SnowAngel:	not EVERYTHING, just . . . everything u'd told me. but come on, we're talking about zoe. she doesn't care!
mad maddie:	**christ. zoe is the last person on earth i wanted to know about this. she already has so many things to feel superior to me about. now she thinks i'm a whore 2.**
SnowAngel:	ur not a whore
mad maddie:	**yeah, just like ur not a lying bitch.**
SnowAngel:	maddie!
mad maddie:	**screw u, angela. go sob to zoe about it and STAY OUT OF MY FUCKING BUSINESS!!!**

Wednesday, November 3, 8:59 PM

SnowAngel:	shit, zoe. shit, shit, shit.
zoegirl:	angela, what's wrong?
SnowAngel:	it slipped out. maddie and i were IMing, and it just slipped out.

Send   Cancel

zoegirl:	what slipped out?
zoegirl:	oh, crap. about the frat party? the fact that we talked?
SnowAngel:	she's really pissed, zoe. she called me a bitch.
zoegirl:	what?!
SnowAngel:	which pisses ME off, but more than that i just feel bad. i didn't mean to make her so upset!
SnowAngel:	oh god, i think i'm gonna throw up.
zoegirl:	angela, relax. it's gonna be ok.
SnowAngel:	i dunno, zoe. she is PISSED.
zoegirl:	should i IM her?
SnowAngel:	not unless u want her to bite your head off.
zoegirl:	it's just that u shouldn't be the only one to have to deal with her. we both messed up, not just u.
SnowAngel:	well, thanks for saying that.
zoegirl:	does she know that we weren't, like, gossiping about her? we were just worried. i mean, she kinda brought this on herself.
SnowAngel:	i told her that, but it didn't go over so well.
zoegirl:	oh
SnowAngel:	*breathe, angela, breathe*
zoegirl:	she was that mad, huh?
SnowAngel:	u wouldn't believe
zoegirl:	well, tomorrow we'll be all humble and apologetic, and she'll calm down. by lunch everything'll be back to normal.
SnowAngel:	ur right, i'm sure ur right. what's she gonna do, give us the silent treatment?
zoegirl:	so go get your beauty sleep (jk) and stop worrying.

Send   Cancel

SnowAngel:	u don't think i'm a horrible person?
zoegirl:	ur not a horrible person.
SnowAngel:	ok
zoegirl:	good nite, angela. don't worry!

Thursday, November 4, 5:38 PM

zoegirl:	hi, maddie. it's me.
mad maddie:	**screw u**
zoegirl:	maddie, come on. ur acting retarded.
mad maddie:	**yep, that's me, miss retarded. thanks for rubbing it in.**
zoegirl:	quit being this way. u wouldn't talk to me in homeroom—thanks a lot—and who knows where u were at lunch. don't u even wanna hear what i have to say?
mad maddie:	**maybe u should rent a billboard. then the whole world would know.**
zoegirl:	look, i'm sorry. i've told u a 100 times. i'm trying to be patient, but this is getting ridiculous.
mad maddie:	**ooo, i'm scared! r u gonna quote the scriptures at me? drag me to church? if i did a striptease in front of a teacher instead of in front of ten million frat boys, would THAT be ok?**
zoegirl:	i'm not gonna talk to u if ur gonna be like this.
mad maddie:	**oh, u wanna "talk," but only on your terms. well here's a newsflash: i don't give a rat's ass. so forget about me and go spin your little fantasies about mr. h, since that's all u ever do anywayz. at least i'm not a stuck-up prude afraid to actually have fun.**
zoegirl:	ur not being fair, maddie.

maddie:	**tell it to angela. u 2 can cry on each other's shoulders and slam me behind my back. but wait, u've already done that, haven't u?**
zoegirl:	that's it. i'm done.
mad maddie:	**boo-fucking-hoo. and in case u missed it the first time around, SCREW U!**

Thursday, November 4, 8:01 PM

SnowAngel:	hey, zoe
zoegirl:	ur home, good
SnowAngel:	yeah, mom said u called. wazzup?
zoegirl:	i tried talking to maddie again—i thought maybe over the computer things would go better—but it was a disaster. she won't listen at all.
SnowAngel:	tell me about it. she's been horrible all day.
zoegirl:	in homeroom, she stalked away right in the middle of my sentence. kristin was like, "what was that all about?" and i couldn't even tell her.
SnowAngel:	i feel bad for her, but she's being a baby.
zoegirl:	it's like she's not even the same maddie.
SnowAngel:	i know
zoegirl:	so what should we do?
SnowAngel:	give her time, i guess. what else can we do?
zoegirl:	i don't know
SnowAngel:	she'll come around. she has to.
SnowAngel:	so . . . r u going to friday morning fellowship tomorrow?
zoegirl:	yeah. i'm, uh, actually leading the prayer. it'll be my first time.

Send   Cancel

SnowAngel:	that's great. good luck.
zoegirl:	thanks. and thanks for not making fun of me.
SnowAngel:	of course 😊
zoegirl:	what about u? did u have fun at drama club?
SnowAngel:	sort of, but mainly i worried about maddie.
zoegirl:	i know what u mean
SnowAngel:	so say a prayer for her tomorrow!
zoegirl:	ha—i will! bye!

Friday, November 5, 6:45 PM

SnowAngel:	hey, mads. r u done being a drama queen yet?

Auto response from mad maddie: everybody was kung fu fighting, those jerks were fast as lightning!

SnowAngel:	maddie, come on. i know ur there.
SnowAngel:	fine!

Friday, November 5, 7:12 PM

zoegirl:	maddie, it's me

Auto response from mad maddie: everybody was kung fu fighting, those jerks were fast as lightning!

zoegirl:	maddie . . . u've at least got to talk to us.
zoegirl:	maddie?
zoegirl:	all right, i'm gonna sign-off now.
zoegirl:	IM me when ur ready to talk!

Friday, November 5, 7:20 PM

zoegirl:	hi, angela. maddie's not responding to my IMs.
SnowAngel:	i know. mine either.

Send   Cancel

zoegirl:	and she didn't say one word to me at school.
SnowAngel:	it's ridiculous. mr. miklos had her pass out the quizzes in geometry, and she slapped one on my desk without even looking at me.
zoegirl:	i wanna shake her and tell her how stupid she's being.
SnowAngel:	me 2. but now she's got her jana friends, so maybe she doesn't need us anymore.
zoegirl:	except jana's cold-shouldering her just like she's cold-shouldering us. haven't u noticed?
SnowAngel:	really? ha. that's kinda funny—only it's not, cuz it's so sad.
zoegirl:	which is why it's doubly stupid that she's turning her back on us. we wouldn't judge her like jana is.
SnowAngel:	she's just being stubborn
SnowAngel:	r u still coming over tonite?
zoegirl:	i'm waiting for mom to finish getting ready, and then she's gonna bring me over.
SnowAngel:	groovy
zoegirl:	but . . . what should we do about maddie?
SnowAngel:	i'll try IMing one more time. if she doesn't answer then it's her own fault.
zoegirl:	ok. c u soon!

Friday, November 5, 7:39 PM

SnowAngel:	hi, madigan. i know ur on-line, so u might as well answer.

Auto response from mad maddie: everybody was kung fu fighting, those jerks were fast as lightning!

Send   Cancel

SnowAngel:	*shakes maddie like a rag doll* ANSWER ME!!!
SnowAngel:	this is getting sooooooooo old, but whatever. anyway, zoe's coming over to spend the nite, and we want u to come 2, even if ur just gonna sit there like a bump on a log. so drive over if u want, ok?
SnowAngel:	*makes megaphone with hands* M-A-D-D-I-E!!!!!
SnowAngel:	well, u know where to find us!

Sunday, November 7, 1:45 PM

zoegirl:	hey, angela
SnowAngel:	hey, zo
zoegirl:	any word from maddie today?
SnowAngel:	nope
zoegirl:	i thought maybe she'd call, since she worked with ian last nite. as far as i know that's the first time she's seen him (or even talked to him) since halloween.
SnowAngel:	yeah, i wonder how that went. i wonder if she was as weird with him as she is with us.
zoegirl:	who knows
SnowAngel:	so how was church this morning?
zoegirl:	it was good
SnowAngel:	good? that's all ur gonna say?
zoegirl:	hmm. i guess i feel strange talking about other stuff with this whole maddie mess going on.
SnowAngel:	why? we DO have lives apart from her, u know.
zoegirl:	true
SnowAngel:	so tell me more! did mr. h finally kiss u? *smooch, smooch*

zoegirl:	yeah, right there at the altar, in front of god and everybody.
SnowAngel:	REALLY?
zoegirl:	angela!
SnowAngel:	well, did u have any romantic moments? meaningful glances, knee-touches, that sort of thing?
zoegirl:	the car ride was nice, even tho we just talked about school. it's so bizarre. it's like there we r, alone in his car with all these vibes bouncing around b/w us, and what do we do? we talk about english and the shakespeare festival and who our favorite authors r.
SnowAngel:	*winks lasciviously* verbal foreplay
zoegirl:	i don't think so
zoegirl:	only . . .
SnowAngel:	what?
zoegirl:	he did mention that he's housesitting for greg kravitz's parents beginning on the 17th. and he also mentioned that the house has an outdoor hot tub.
SnowAngel:	omg. AND?
zoegirl:	and he kinda hinted around that maybe i could come over one nite, and we could gaze at the stars.
SnowAngel:	IN the hot tub, IN your bathing suits! OR—*gasp!*— MAYBE IN YOUR NUDEY PANTS!!!!
zoegirl:	god, angela! ur making me blush. we will not be in our "nudey pants," thank u very much. he hasn't even technically invited me!
SnowAngel:	well when he does, will u say yes?
zoegirl:	i don't know. it makes me nervous just thinking about it.
SnowAngel:	good nervous or bad nervous?

Send   Cancel

zoegirl:	i don't know!
zoegirl:	ack, now my palms r all sweaty. can we talk about something else, please?
SnowAngel:	sure. have u picked which swimsuit ur gonna wear yet?
zoegirl:	angela!
SnowAngel:	not your blue one-piece. it comes up to, like, your collar bone. and not that nasty red one with the worn spots in the butt, altho i suppose that could work to your advantage . . .
zoegirl:	enuff
SnowAngel:	u'll have to borrow my pink 2-piece—that's all there is to it. and u should probably go to a tanning salon. otherwise u'll look like a dead codfish, no offense.
zoegirl:	if i wore your pink 2-piece, it would fall right off me. (and stop right there with what ur thinking!) and i'm not going to a tanning salon. god.
SnowAngel:	hey, u asked for my advice
zoegirl:	no, i didn't
SnowAngel:	well u should have
zoegirl:	am i really 2 pale to wear a bathing suit?
SnowAngel:	it's november—of course ur pale. i am 2, altho it hardly matters since i'm not going hot-tubbing with my lusty young buck of an english teacher.
zoegirl:	oh god, i think i'm gonna faint.
SnowAngel:	u can always use tanning creme if u don't wanna go to a tanning booth. just don't turn yourself orange.
zoegirl:	i'm gonna go now, angela.

	ttyl

SnowAngel: but we haven't even discussed your thong possibilities! yikes, u better start doing your butt exercises. *squeeze and lift and squeeze and lift and pump and pump and pump!*

zoegirl: good-bye!!!

Monday, November 8, 9:21 PM

SnowAngel: hey, zoe girl

zoegirl: hey, angela

SnowAngel: any luck with maddie today?

zoegirl: no, u?

SnowAngel: she shot me a death look when i tried to talk to her in geometry. does that count?

zoegirl: maddie does give a good death look, i'll give her that.

SnowAngel: so, not to be self-absorbed or anything, but does this mean our cumberland island trip is off? thanksgiving's only 2 and a half weeks away.

zoegirl: i've been wondering about that 2. maddie was so psyched about it.

SnowAngel: then she should get off her high horse and stop being sullen!

SnowAngel: hey, check it out. she's on-line. i'm gonna IM her and ask about our trip.

zoegirl: seriously?

SnowAngel: why not? even if she doesn't reply, i can at least make her feel guilty about it. it's not fair for her to back out now.

zoegirl: i hope she answers. good luck!

Send   Cancel

Monday, November 8, 9:42 PM

SnowAngel: hey, madikins. it's me, angela.

Auto response from mad maddie: everybody was kung fu fighting, those jerks were fast as lightning!

SnowAngel: aw, maddie, give me a break. u just popped up on my buddy list, so i know ur there.

SnowAngel: fine, i'll talk AT u, then. zoe and i wanna know about our trip to cumberland island. we've been planning it for so long, and it was gonna be sooooooo much fun. r we still on or not?

SnowAngel: i GUESS we could go even if ur stonewalling us, but that would make for a pretty dreadful car ride. i can c it now: u alone in the front, scowling and clutching the steering wheel, while zoe and i cower in the back, begging u to give us a potty break. (that was a joke)

SnowAngel: *sigh*

SnowAngel: well, talk to us when ur ready then. only u better not wait 2 long, cuz who knows? we might make other plans. we don't wanna, tho, so stop sulking and talk to us!!!!

Monday, November 8, 9:50 PM

SnowAngel: oh, maddie? one more thing.

Auto response from mad maddie: everybody was kung fu fighting, those jerks were fast as lightning!

SnowAngel: CHANGE YOUR STUPID AUTO RESPONSE! IT'S DRIVING ME NUTS!

Tuesday, November 9, 5:23 PM

zoegirl:	shit, angela. guess who just called me?
SnowAngel:	hi to u 2, zoe. who, maddie?!!
zoegirl:	i wish. no, nealie anderson.
SnowAngel:	nealie anderson? she says her "s"s weird. why'd she call?
zoegirl:	cuz she's kinda friends with terri springer, and apparently terri just got an awful email from jana. well, nealie thought it was awful. terri thought it was hysterical.
SnowAngel:	oh, no
SnowAngel:	did it have to do with maddie?
zoegirl:	jana sent pictures, angela. she sent out an email with pics from that frat party. they were of maddie dancing on the table, and she was naked from the waist up.
SnowAngel:	SHIT. someone took pictures?
zoegirl:	apparently so. and apparently it was jana.
SnowAngel:	I HATE HER!!!
zoegirl:	the subject line was "lesbo slut." terri forwarded nealie the message. she forwarded it to, like, the entire school.
SnowAngel:	shit, shit, SHIT.
SnowAngel:	did u ask her to forward it to u?
zoegirl:	NO!
SnowAngel:	god, why now? why did jana do this NOW, a fucking week later?
zoegirl:	who knows. why does jana do ANYTHING she does?
zoegirl:	maybe she just got her film back. maybe she's sick of maddie's hangdog looks and wanted to screw her for good.

Send   Cancel

SnowAngel:	oh, god. does maddie know?
zoegirl:	i don't know. that's why nealie called me, tho, cuz she knows maddie's my friend.
SnowAngel:	used to be, at any rate
zoegirl:	u know what i mean. anyway, maddie still is my friend even if i'm no longer hers.
SnowAngel:	i know. i'm just in shock. i just can't believe anyone would do something like that, even jana.
SnowAngel:	should we tell her? maddie, i mean?
zoegirl:	i don't know
SnowAngel:	maybe she won't find out. maybe no one'll mention it.
zoegirl:	yeah, that's likely
SnowAngel:	well what r we supposed to do, then?
zoegirl:	i have no clue
zoegirl:	maybe we should just, like, stick close tomorrow, so we can be there if something does happen.
SnowAngel:	ok, yeah
zoegirl:	we'll know more tomorrow, after we c what happens. and like u said, maybe it'll all blow over.
SnowAngel:	*crosses fingers*
zoegirl:	bye, angela
SnowAngel:	bye, zo. i'm glad nealie called u.
zoegirl:	yeah, me 2. (i guess)

Tuesday, November 9, 10:09 PM

zoegirl:	maddie?
Auto response from mad maddie: shove it up your ass	
zoegirl:	what?

177

zoegirl:	just wanted to let u know i'm here. that's all.

Wednesday, November 10, 8:45 PM

SnowAngel:	hey, zo
zoegirl:	hey, angela
SnowAngel:	no call from maddie, just so u know. not that i should have expected it, i suppose, but after what happened in geometry, i thought she'd at least want a shoulder to cry on.
zoegirl:	well, she probably does, but for whatever reason, she doesn't think she can come to us.
SnowAngel:	BUT WE'VE BEEN BEST FRIENDS FOR 4 YEARS!!! who else is she supposed to go to?
zoegirl:	i know, i know
SnowAngel:	i just don't get it, zoe. it broke my heart to c her striding down the halls with her lips all clamped together. it's gotta be killing her. u'd think she'd WANT her friends around her at a time like this. or that she'd at least wanna TALK to us about it!
zoegirl:	maybe it's a pride thing. like, now that everyone knows what happened, she's determined to hold her head up and pretend she doesn't give a damn.
SnowAngel:	tough to do when ppl r asking how much she charges for a private party.
zoegirl:	god, i can't even imagine
SnowAngel:	and what does mr. miklos do? he just stands there blinking and rubbing his neck, saying, "class, class! could we bring it down to a dull roar?" he had no clue.

Send   Cancel

zoegirl:	well, it's bad enuff the students know. if mr. miklos knew, or any other teacher, they'd probably send maddie to counseling.
SnowAngel:	*shudders*
zoegirl:	what about maddie's parents—do u think they know?
SnowAngel:	they were off at some party when she came home that nite, so they don't know about that part. and i'm sure she hasn't told them anything more.
SnowAngel:	oh god, can u think of anything worse?
zoegirl:	if it were me, can u imagine what my mom would do?
SnowAngel:	it's lucky mark's out of high school, or he'd have heard about it and told them. so MAYBE she's safe. *cross your fingers*
SnowAngel:	did u c jana after school let out, sitting on the steps with terri and jane olsen?
zoegirl:	no, what did they do?
SnowAngel:	they were just hanging out, laffing and joking around like "la-di-da, isn't life great." in my head i was like, "u bitch! don't u know that u've ruined someone's life?! don't u even care?" but of course she doesn't, or she wouldn't have sent that email. she gets off on other ppl's pain.
zoegirl:	u were right from the beginning, angela. she's evil.
SnowAngel:	one good thing: it's all downhill for her from here. i was talking to mom about her last nite—not the specifics, just in general—and mom said that girls like jana peak in high school, then wonder why the rest of their lives seem so rotten. just wait, we'll c jana at our 10th reunion and she'll be fat

179

and pathetic. she'll work at wal-mart and wear a horrid blue smock.

zoegirl:	yeah
SnowAngel:	nothing like seeing the mega-cools turn into mega-drools. she SO has it coming to her.
zoegirl:	i wish someone would send around pics of her doing something embarrassing, u know? i mean, she's done so much worse than what maddie did. but cuz she's the kind of person she is, she's the one who always makes everyone else look bad.
SnowAngel:	i know. listen, i'm gonna try maddie again. i know she probably won't talk, but i've got to do something.
zoegirl:	ok. bye!

Wednesday, November 10, 9:15 PM

SnowAngel:	hi, maddie. it's me.

Auto response from mad maddie: shove it up your ass

SnowAngel:	oh, that's nice. real mature. i liked the kung fu better, believe it or not.
SnowAngel:	anyway, i just wanted to let u know that i luv u. zoe 2. we're still your friends, even if u don't think so.
SnowAngel:	call me if u wanna talk!!!!!

Thursday, November 11, 10:01 PM

SnowAngel:	hey, zo. remember in 8th grade when my parents rented that house at myrtle beach, and u and maddie got to come 2? and we had that contest to c who could eat the most banana pudding?
zoegirl:	and the only thing we could wash it down with was fanta

	grape, and afterward maddie looked pregnant cuz she'd eaten so much. what made u think of that?
SnowAngel:	nothing, i guess. i was just thinking about all the stuff we've done together.
zoegirl:	yeah
zoegirl:	i know what u mean

Friday, November 12, 5:05 PM

zoegirl:	hey, angela
SnowAngel:	hey, zo. wazzup?
zoegirl:	well, i was hoping i could talk to u about something that doesn't have to do with maddie, if that's ok.
SnowAngel:	of course
zoegirl:	it has to do with mr. h.
SnowAngel:	ahh, intrigue
zoegirl:	shut up, it's not THAT exciting. but this morning at friday morning fellowship, he said something that sort of weirded me out.
SnowAngel:	were u 2 alone, or with the whole group?
zoegirl:	everyone else was there, but we were sitting at the far end of the table and no one was paying attention to us. altho actually that made it even creepier, that he would say something like that in a room full of other ppl.
SnowAngel:	*bams on computer desk* what did he say?!!
zoegirl:	he was talking about next weekend, which is when he's gonna be housesitting for the kravitzes, and at first it was, like, sexy that he would bring it up with everyone else around. (don't laff!)
SnowAngel:	i'm not laffing. but what do u mean?

zoegirl:	just that nobody was listening, but they COULD have been. and that made it . . . i don't know. exciting.
SnowAngel:	oh, man
zoegirl:	he told me about the kravitzes' house, how nice it was, and he told me about the hot tub again. and then he lowered his voice and said, "ur still coming, right?"
SnowAngel:	ooo, it gets ME excited. what'd u say?
zoegirl:	i said, "i think so, yeah," and he said, "good." then he touched my hand really lightly and said, "u can wear your bikini."
SnowAngel:	!!!
zoegirl:	at first i thought he was just teasing me, and i said, "yeah, right, me in a bikini. wouldn't that be a lovely sight."
SnowAngel:	*tsk, tsk* u'd look great in a bikini.
zoegirl:	i don't even own one. anyway, that's not the point. the point is that his eyes kinda dipped over my body, and he said, "it would indeed be a lovely sight. i've been looking forward to it."
SnowAngel:	"it would indeed"?!!
zoegirl:	i know. it sounded fake, almost like a come on. altho i know that's silly, cuz why would he hit on me?
SnowAngel:	zoe, u have got to get over this humble-pie thing and OPEN YOUR EYES. he IS hitting on u. MR. H IS HITTING ON U. the question is, what r u gonna do about it?
zoegirl:	i don't know. i'm flattered, i guess. but all of a sudden it feels . . . REAL. in a physical bodies kinda way and not just as a meeting of the minds.

Send   Cancel

SnowAngel:	only u would talk about your affair as a "meeting of the minds."
zoegirl:	it's not an affair.
SnowAngel:	not yet . . .
zoegirl:	anyway, my stomach's in knots, and whenever i think about next weekend, i feel like i'm gonna throw up.
SnowAngel:	don't worry, ur just nervous.
zoegirl:	but is that a good thing? i keep thinking, what if i knew that some 24-year-old was interested in u? i'd wonder what was wrong with him.
SnowAngel:	*splutters in outrage* thanks a lot!
zoegirl:	u know what i mean. i'm 15. he's 9 years older than me—and he's my teacher.
SnowAngel:	ur just now realizing this?
zoegirl:	no. i'm just now admitting that maybe it's a little sketchy.
SnowAngel:	so ur not gonna go hot tubbing with him?
zoegirl:	i never said that
SnowAngel:	so u R gonna go hot tubbing with him?
zoegirl:	i never said that either, altho as far as he knows, i am. but if i do, i'm not wearing a bikini.
SnowAngel:	u should wear one of those granny suits, one of those old-timey ones that covers up your entire body. or wear one of those bathing suits with a skirt. ha!
zoegirl:	ack, this is not helping
SnowAngel:	well, u don't have to make up your mind right this second.

183

zoegirl:	i wish i could talk to maddie about it, even tho i know she'd just make fun of me. but maybe that's what i need, u know?
SnowAngel:	yeah
SnowAngel:	did u hear what happened in 6th period, how brant simms offered her ten bucks for a peep show?
zoegirl:	what an asshole
zoegirl:	how'd u hear that?
SnowAngel:	a couple of kids were talking about it in history. they shut up when i sat down.
zoegirl:	god, poor maddie
SnowAngel:	i saw her walking to her car when i was on my way to drama club. her eyes were all puffy. i called out to her, but of course she didn't turn around.
zoegirl:	aargh
SnowAngel:	i miss her, zoe ☹
zoegirl:	me 2
SnowAngel:	crap. mom's calling me to come set the table.
zoegirl:	bye!

Saturday, November 13, 10:30 AM

SnowAngel:	zoe—i have an awesome idea!
zoegirl:	oh yeah?
SnowAngel:	let's make maddie a care package! *claps excitedly*
zoegirl:	to cheer her up, u mean?
SnowAngel:	exactamundo. we could decorate a box and fill it with candy and tacky magazines and stuff like that.
zoegirl:	hmm. and we could write her a sappy poem telling her how much we miss her.

184

SnowAngel:	perfect
SnowAngel:	altho u'll have to write it since i suck at that stuff.
zoegirl:	maybe we could take a picture of the 2 of us looking sad and forlorn. hey, i know—we could have our arms over each other's shoulders, and then one of us could have her other arm out in the air, around the place maddie would be if she were there. it'll show, like, the gap she's left in our friendship. how we aren't whole without her.
SnowAngel:	ooo, ur good. get your mom to bring u over, and we can walk to king's and go shopping.
zoegirl:	how will we get the care package to her once we've made it? will we actually mail it?
SnowAngel:	nah, that would take 2 long. we'll just leave it on her doorstep and run.
zoegirl:	i'll c if mom can drop me off. if u don't hear back from me, that means i'm on my way. bye!

Saturday, November 13, 6:12 PM

zoegirl:	hey, angela. how did it go when u dropped off maddie's box? sorry i had to leave so early!
SnowAngel:	at least u got to help me put everything together. oh, and your poem was fabulous. *strikes pose* *u r our buddy, our buddy to stay, til ur all dried up and peeled away.*
zoegirl:	that part was from an old garfield comic about a dead toad. i can't take credit.
SnowAngel:	who cares, it's funny. and it's perfect for maddie cuz it's mushy but not 2 mushy. she'll luv it.
zoegirl:	so did u c her when u delivered it? was she at home?

Send   Cancel

185

SnowAngel:	she was, cuz i saw her in the living room, peering at me from behind the curtains. i thought for a minute she was gonna come out, especially when she figured out what i was doing, but she didn't.
zoegirl:	damn
SnowAngel:	but maybe our care package will be just the thing. she can't hold out 4ever.
zoegirl:	i sure hope not. anyway, way 2 go!
SnowAngel:	thanks!

Sunday, November 14, 1:35 PM

SnowAngel:	finally! i've been waiting and waiting for u to get home. did u get my message?
zoegirl:	hi, angela. i did, and i tried calling u back, but i got your voice mail. do u EVER remember to leave your phone turned on?
zoegirl:	anyway, what's up?
SnowAngel:	what do u mean, what's up? TELL ME HOW CHURCH WAS!
zoegirl:	oh, that
SnowAngel:	did mr. h talk about your bikini again? did he make any moves when u were in the car together?
zoegirl:	i got mom to drop me off and pick me up. i thought about riding all that way with him and got freaked out.
SnowAngel:	why'd u even go, then?
zoegirl:	well, i do like the church service. i honestly do. and i was worried what he'd think if i just didn't show.
SnowAngel:	oh
SnowAngel:	so did he say anything at all?

zoegirl:	he told me he liked my dress. he whispered it really softly during one of the hymns.
SnowAngel:	hmm. was he being creepy or cute?
zoegirl:	i don't know. both? cute, mainly, but i get scared at the thought of being alone with him.
SnowAngel:	uh, zoe? *flicks zoe's head with finger* hate to break it to u, but if ur scared to be alone with a guy, that's called creepy. i think it's time to cut this one loose, soldier.
zoegirl:	but what am i supposed to tell him? he bought sparkling apple juice for us and everything!
SnowAngel:	WHAT?!!
zoegirl:	woops. i wasn't gonna mention that.
SnowAngel:	mr. h bought sparkling apple juice for your big hot-tubbing date? that is so dorky i think i'm gonna cry.
zoegirl:	he's gonna get strawberries and chocolate 2, only i'm pretty sure i don't wanna go anymore.
zoegirl:	help!
SnowAngel:	this is crazy, zo
zoegirl:	i know
SnowAngel:	want me to call the school board?
zoegirl:	omg, don't even say that. he would be so dead. and so would i!
SnowAngel:	don't worry. i was kidding.
zoegirl:	anyway, he trusts me. he would freak if he knew i'd told anybody, even u.
SnowAngel:	but c'mon, what is he thinking? that it's normal to be hitting on a 15-year-old student?

Send   Cancel

ttyl	

zoegirl: it's my fault for going to backwork all those times. i gave him the wrong idea.

SnowAngel: u don't seriously believe that, do u?

zoegirl: kinda

SnowAngel: first of all, u didn't give him the "wrong" idea, cuz up til now u've totally been crushing on him and u know it.

zoegirl: i know, which is why i feel so bad.

SnowAngel: but second of all, HE'S the grown-up. if it's anybody's fault, it's his.

zoegirl: i don't want it to be anyone's fault. i just want it to be over.

SnowAngel: so tell him

zoegirl: but what if i'm wrong? what if he just, u know, wants to talk about the Bible?

SnowAngel: *snorts*

zoegirl: anyway, everything'll be fine. i'll think of something and it'll all be fine.

SnowAngel: if u say so

zoegirl: i'm gonna go now. i've got to do some homework. but real quick: any word from maddie?

SnowAngel: if there was, i would have told u.

zoegirl: well, maybe tomorrow. bye!

Monday, November 15, 5:24 PM

SnowAngel: o. m. g. if i hear one more joke about maddie and the gold club or maddie charging admission or maddie being a titty-tease, i'm gonna scream.

zoegirl: i know. think how awful it must be for maddie. over the

Send   Cancel

weekend she can forget about it for a while, but then on monday she has to plod right back and deal with it all over again.

SnowAngel: i'm surprised she comes at all. i'd stay at home with a mysterious illness.

zoegirl: for an entire week? anyway, she'd have to face everyone eventually. she couldn't skip 4ever.

SnowAngel: i could. i'd flee to a convent and become a nun.

zoegirl: u would be a terrible nun.

SnowAngel: what r u talking about? i look good in black. i'd just have to do away with that headdress thing they wear.

zoegirl: it's called a wimple

SnowAngel: god, even the name is dreadful. *pretends to be a nun: excuse me while i put on my pimple—i mean dimple—i mean wimple!*

zoegirl: don't be a nun, angela.

SnowAngel: *waves away zoe's foolishness*

SnowAngel: oh, and u want to hear something really lovely?

zoegirl: what?

SnowAngel: maddie was late to geometry, and there were only 2 seats left, one next to me and one next to barry beryl. guess which one she picked?

zoegirl: oh god, not barry. really?

SnowAngel: yes, it's true. she chose barry "the sneeze" beryl over her best friend since 7th grade. namely, me.

zoegirl: that's so wrong

SnowAngel: i know. hey, i'm gonna go, but i'll call u l8r. or u call me. bye!

Monday, November 15, 7:30 PM

SnowAngel:	maddie's not really gonna ditch us 4ever, right? i mean, deep inside she's still the same maddie, and she knows we're still the same angela and zoe. right?
zoegirl:	i don't know, angela. i thought she would have come around a long time ago.
SnowAngel:	yeah, me 2
SnowAngel:	THIS IS SO MESSED UP!!!

Tuesday, November 16, 8:01 PM

SnowAngel:	zoe! guess what?!!
zoegirl:	hold on, i've got one convo going with megan and another with kristin. they're both pissed at each other for no good reason.
SnowAngel:	well, tell them to IM each other and talk it over, cuz i've got to tell u my news. BEN SCHLANKER ASKED ME OUT! *squeals and dances about*
zoegirl:	ben asked u out? how did THIS happen?
SnowAngel:	today at drama club he made an announcement about this poetry slam at the coffee connection tomorrow nite, and he invited us all to come.
zoegirl:	this counts as asking u out?
SnowAngel:	yes, cuz even tho he was talking to the whole room, he looked right at me when he said it. *shakes booty in sexy circles*
zoegirl:	uh, ok
zoegirl:	what's a poetry slam?
SnowAngel:	it's when a bunch of ppl get up and read their

Send   Cancel

	poems, and everyone gets a score from 1 to 10. the audience boos or cheers to help the judges decide, and the winner gets, like, fifty dollars and a free pizza.
zoegirl:	and this is something u wanna attend?
SnowAngel:	don't u think it sounds fun?
zoegirl:	actually, yeah. i'm just surprised u do.
SnowAngel:	ye of little faith. i adore poetry.
zoegirl:	mmm-hmm
zoegirl:	ha. now kristin's saying that megan forgot to wait for her at lunch, which is so ironic. kristin takes off without megan all the time.
SnowAngel:	PAY ATTENTION! let us play pretend starring moi and ben schlanker. there we r at coffee connection, sipping our cappuccinos and having an extremely sophisticated conversation about . . . about . . .
zoegirl:	coffee?
SnowAngel:	about ART. and ben looks into my eyes, which r as blue as a summer sky, and says, "oh, angela, your eyes r as blue as a summer sky."
zoegirl:	ack
SnowAngel:	and then he cradles my face in his hand, like he's protecting me from the harsh reality of life, and plants a big smackeroo on my eagerly parted lips.
zoegirl:	and the judges raise their cards to show a unanimous score of 10! and the coffee house goes wild with applause!
SnowAngel:	of course for this fantasy to come true, i first have to decide what to wear.

Send   Cancel

zoegirl:	how about some clothes?
SnowAngel:	no time for jokes! must go ransack my closet!

Wednesday, November 17, 5:45 PM

SnowAngel:	la la la, la la la, only one more hour til my date with ben!
zoegirl:	u sure u wanna go thru this again, angela?
SnowAngel:	go thru what?
zoegirl:	never mind
zoegirl:	so r u IMing to describe your lovely, gussied-up self?
SnowAngel:	*clears throat* attire: black cords, betty boop t-shirt, dark blue jean jacket, maroon doc martens, silver i.d. bracelet. scent: my mom's "chance" by coco chanel.
zoegirl:	very nice. very hip.
SnowAngel:	yeah? i considered borrowing chrissy's black coat with the faux fur trim, but decided it might be 2 much.
zoegirl:	good call
SnowAngel:	what i really wanna borrow is maddie's bottlecap belt. she took it back after the last time i wore it, tho, and i don't think i can call up and ask for it.
zoegirl:	probably not
zoegirl:	then again, who knows? maybe it'd be a good icebreaker.
SnowAngel:	maybe
SnowAngel:	but nah, i'm not up for rejection right now. it would bum me out.
SnowAngel:	is it bad that i'm so excited while maddie's still so miserable?

zoegirl:	well, ur not excited cuz she's miserable. they're 2 different things. and u can't put your life on hold 4ever.
SnowAngel:	that's true
zoegirl:	maybe we should do something else to do to cheer her up, tho. give her a chance to come back.
SnowAngel:	only we've already given her lots of chances, and she hasn't taken any of them.
SnowAngel:	aye-yai-yai, it's 6:15 and everyone's meeting at the coffee house at 6:45. that's only half an hour away! *quick kiss and a hug for good luck* BYE!

Wednesday, November 17, 10:15 PM

SnowAngel:	hiya, zo. well, i'm back from my hot poetry date. NOT.
zoegirl:	uh oh. what happened?
SnowAngel:	let's c, how should i put it? BEN SHOWED UP WITH LESLIE.
SnowAngel:	there, i said it.
zoegirl:	who's leslie?
SnowAngel:	that GA state chick he's always talking about. the girl i convinced myself was just a friend. remember?
zoegirl:	i take it she's not?
SnowAngel:	she wore a hideous pearl necklace, one that looped around twice and still hung down to her belly button.
SnowAngel:	how could he go out with her when he could have had ME?
zoegirl:	ah, angela
SnowAngel:	it's so unfair!

Send   Cancel

ttyl	

zoegirl: maybe it's just as well. u've seen the kinda trouble u can get in with an older man.

SnowAngel: she, like, rubbed his neck the whole time we were there. it was disgusting. ☺

zoegirl: what about the poetry slam itself? was it fun?

SnowAngel: hmm. where do i start? ben read one of his poems—after prying himself from leslie's claws—and it was BAD. it was about rebirth or resurrection or something, and i could tell from the way he read it that it was supposed to be really deep.

zoegirl: but it wasn't?

SnowAngel: at the end he pretended to be an egg. he scrunched into a ball with his arms wrapped around his legs and stayed like that, frozen, while everyone clapped.

zoegirl: oh good heavens

SnowAngel: my crush has been nipped in the bud. or, shall i say, my crush has been scrambled, fried, and poached.

SnowAngel: tee-hee. that was funny, wasn't it?

zoegirl: at least ur in a good humor about it.

SnowAngel: well . . . the nite wasn't TOTALLY bunk.

zoegirl: oh yeah?

SnowAngel: prepare yourself for another bombshell: doug schmidt was there.

zoegirl: doug schmidt? i didn't know he was in the drama club.

SnowAngel: he's not. he came on his own.

zoegirl: cuz he knew u were gonna be there?

SnowAngel: no, he came to compete in the poetry slam. he

Send Cancel

	read a poem about dirty underwear, which sounds gross, but it was really funny. UNLIKE mr. deep's stupid egg poem.
zoegirl:	huh
SnowAngel:	and afterward, he and i sat together and drank chai milkshakes while leslie caressed ben's hair. doug told me he wants to be a writer when he grows up, but that he would never take himself 2 seriously. it was cool, cuz there's like so much more to him than i thought.
zoegirl:	so . . . is he your new crush?
SnowAngel:	what? no!!! i have fun hanging out with him, but he is NOT my type.
zoegirl:	yeah, like that's ever stopped u.
SnowAngel:	what r u talking about? u really lose me sometimes.
zoegirl:	oh, angela. i'm glad u had fun, that's all.
SnowAngel:	me 2. nite!

Thursday, November 18, 5:00 PM

SnowAngel:	hey, zo. i saw u talking to mr. h in the hall after 5th period. he was looking VERY interested in what u have to say.
zoegirl:	we were talking about the quiz he gave in class, so shut up.
SnowAngel:	well, he was rapt. have u figured out what ur gonna do about this weekend?
zoegirl:	aargh! i haven't! and every time i think about it, i get all jittery and i have to do jumping-jacks to calm down.
SnowAngel:	ur gonna have to come up with something. time's a' tickin.

zoegirl:	i KNOW. he's expecting me at the kravitzes' TOMORROW NITE!!!
SnowAngel:	know who could tell u what to do? maddie, cuz she's so good at cutting through the bullshit.
zoegirl:	god, ur right
SnowAngel:	u should IM her
zoegirl:	maybe i will
SnowAngel:	do it! i'm gonna get off so u can.
zoegirl:	it's worth a try, i guess.
SnowAngel:	i'm getting off, so call me if she responds! bye!

Thursday, November 18, 5:19 PM

zoegirl:	maddie, r u there?

Auto response from mad maddie: shove it up your ass

zoegirl:	maddie, i need to talk to u. please?
zoegirl:	it's about mr. h.
zoegirl:	he wants me to go hot-tubbing with him, and i don't know what to do.
zoegirl:	maddie?
zoegirl:	ok. well, i really could have used your advice, but i guess u don't care!

Friday, November 19, 10:09 AM

zoegirl:	angela! thank god!
SnowAngel:	zoe? what r u doing on-line?
zoegirl:	i saw tammy in the hall, and she said mr. kirk was taking your class to the library to do research. thank god, cuz i really need to talk to u.

Send   Cancel

SnowAngel:	where r u? why aren't u in class?
zoegirl:	i'm in ms. phillip's office. i do my student aide stuff this period, remember?
SnowAngel:	she doesn't care if u use her computer?
zoegirl:	she's never here. she slaps down a stack of quizzes for me to grade, then goes outside to smoke.
SnowAngel:	oh. well, wazzup?
zoegirl:	i am so dead! i saw mr. h at fellowship this morning—i was 2 wimpy not to go—and when we were in the kitchen getting our orange juice, he said, "i'm looking forward to tonite. i got a special candle just for the occasion."
SnowAngel:	ew! ick, ick, ick!
zoegirl:	he said it in this shy little boy way, and it would have been cute if i'd still been into him. but i'm not!!!
SnowAngel:	did u tell him u couldn't come?
zoegirl:	no! i said something brilliant like, "uh, great," and then i darted off to get a sweet roll—not that i was able to eat it. i wanted to tell him no, but i just couldn't!
SnowAngel:	zoe, u have to get out of it.
zoegirl:	but how? he's coming to pick me up at 7. i already told mom i'm going to bible study with him, like years ago before i got freaked out, and she's delighted. she'll probably have a plate of cookies for him when he arrives.
SnowAngel:	well, what if u told her the truth?
zoegirl:	r u KIDDING? that would be a disaster. omg, she'd call the entire school board. and then she'd realize i'd been lying to her all this time and she'd—shit, i have no idea what she'd do. but it would be BAD!

SnowAngel:	ok, ur right. scratch that.
SnowAngel:	maybe u could get sick?
zoegirl:	i suck at faking that stuff. u know that.
SnowAngel:	it's cuz ur such a goody-goody. u haven't had enuff practice.
SnowAngel:	maybe u could just not be there when he comes to pick u up?
zoegirl:	where would i be, in a closet? anyway, there's still the mom problem cuz she knows i've got plans with him. i can't just disappear.
SnowAngel:	i could
zoegirl:	well, i can't!
SnowAngel:	all right, all right. no need to get testy.
zoegirl:	my stomach's in knots. i keep imagining these horrible scenarios with the 2 of us alone in the kravitzes' hot tub. what do i do if he actually tries something?
SnowAngel:	u say, "no!" and if he KEEPS trying, u slap his face and say, "no means no, u weirdo stalkerhead!"
zoegirl:	oh thank u, that's very helpful.
SnowAngel:	or i know! u could say, "now, now. what would jesus do?"
zoegirl:	stop joking!
SnowAngel:	i'm sorry, i'm sorry! it's just that now I'M all anxious, and i don't know what else to do!
zoegirl:	great. this is just great.
SnowAngel:	shit, here comes mr. kirk. i think he's been telling us to go to some site about shakespeare, which of course i haven't. g2g!
zoegirl:	ANGELA!!!

Friday, November 19, 6:45 PM

SnowAngel:	MADDIE, I NEED TO TALK TO U! THIS IS **SERIOUS!!!**

Auto response from mad maddie: shove it up your ass

SnowAngel:	MADDIE!!!
SnowAngel:	i know ur there, so i'm gonna tell u anyway. i just got off the phone with zoe, and i'm totally freaked. she's on her way to greg kravitz's house with mr. h—the kravitzes r out of town, it's a long story—and mr. h thinks she's gonna go hot-tubbing with him. he showed up at the door while we were talking, and maddie, her voice got all panicky and she hung up really quick. WE HAVE TO DO SOMETHING!!!
SnowAngel:	maddie!!! we're talking about zoe, who can't say no to anyone. straight A, honor student, ppl-pleasing zoe. do u understand how serious this is?
SnowAngel:	fine, i'll just figure something out myself. only i have no idea what to do and i can't stop thinking about it and if u were really her friend u'd help me. IF ANYTHING HAPPENS, HER BLOOD WILL BE ON YOUR SHOULDERS!!!
mad maddie:	**her blood will be on my SHOULDERS? god, ur dramatic.**
SnowAngel:	maddie! thank god!
mad maddie:	**anywayz, her blood would be on my HANDS, not dripping down my shoulders like in some scary eyeball horror movie.**
SnowAngel:	whatever. so what r we gonna do?
mad maddie:	**u said they're going to the kravitzes'?**
SnowAngel:	uh-huh

mad maddie:	then so r we. i'll pick u up in ten minutes.
SnowAngel:	yes yes yes!
mad maddie:	and grab your swimsuit. dunno about u, but i'm in the mood to go hot-tubbing.
SnowAngel:	UR WONDERFUL!!! BYE!

Saturday, November 20, 10:35 AM

SnowAngel:	hi, dear, sweet maddie 😊
mad maddie:	**hi, angela**
SnowAngel:	have i told u how awesome u r yet this morning?
mad maddie:	**not unless u airmailed it.**
SnowAngel:	well, u r. *warm fuzzies for the mads, queen of heroic rescues*
mad maddie:	**whatevs**
mad maddie:	**we pulled it off, tho, huh?**
SnowAngel:	hell yeah! i keep seeing mr. h's face when we came through the back gate, how he went from shocked to scared to "i'm cool, i'm cool" in, like, five seconds.
mad maddie:	**it was classic**
SnowAngel:	and zoe, how her eyes were like total saucers. especially when u stepped into the hot tub in that hideous purple tank.
mad maddie:	**it was the only one i could find. i ordered it from j. crew last summer, but i never wore it cuz it's so ugly.**
SnowAngel:	it made u look like a bruise
mad maddie:	**well i, for one, had a marvelous time. so nice, lounging in a hot tub in the middle of november.**
SnowAngel:	oh yes, we should do it more often.

Send   Cancel

mad maddie: i'll mention it to mr. h. maybe we can squeeze something in next weekend.

SnowAngel: hahahahaha! the winsome threesome strikes again! 😎

SnowAngel: i say we go to shoney's breakfast bar to celebrate. u game?

mad maddie: i dunno, angela

SnowAngel: mmm, bacon. mmm, those fiendishly good french toast sticks.

mad maddie: ok, u convinced me

SnowAngel: *pirouettes gleefully*

mad maddie: u gonna IM zoe?

SnowAngel: u do it

mad maddie: why me?

SnowAngel: u know why. last nite was all razzle-dazzle and hysteria—and it was glorious—but i could tell there was still weirdness b/w u 2. zoe loves u and u luv zoe, but u need to officially clear the air.

mad maddie: oh, please

SnowAngel: want me to set up a chat room? then i'd be there to give u moral support, since ur scared to IM her on your own.

mad maddie: don't set up a chat room. it would make me self-conscious.

mad maddie: and no, i'm not scared to IM her. god.

SnowAngel: so u'll do it, then?

mad maddie: fine

SnowAngel: atta girl!

mad maddie: whatevs. i'll pick u up in half an hour!

| Send | Cancel | | 201 |

Saturday, November 20, 11:04 AM

mad maddie: **hey, zo. it's me, maddie.**

mad maddie: **well, duh. obviously it's me, unless someone stole my screen name.**

zoegirl: hi, mads. i was just gonna IM u.

mad maddie: **yeah, sure**

mad maddie: **so wazzup?**

zoegirl: nothing much. u?

mad maddie: **just chillin**

zoegirl: well, u deserve 2. thanks, u know, for last nite

mad maddie: **tell me about it. i saved your butt good didn't i? i can't believe u let yourself be alone with him—and in a HOT TUB no less.**

zoegirl: oh, great

zoegirl: i tell u thanks and all u do is rub it in how stupid i was.

mad maddie: **well u have to admit u were. what the hell were u thinking?**

zoegirl: oh that's lovely, that really makes me feel better.

zoegirl: anyway, i would think that u of all ppl would understand.

mad maddie: **excuse me? what is THAT supposed to mean?**

mad maddie: **anywayz, i think that U of all ppl would be the slightest bit grateful for being rescued! i wasn't that lucky, but U were!**

zoegirl: oh my god. why r we doing this?

mad maddie: **i have no idea. angela said things were weird b/w us, and i guess she was right.**

zoegirl: i guess so

mad maddie: **fine**

zoegirl: fine

Send   Cancel

mad maddie:	**FINE!**
zoegirl:	FINE!
zoegirl:	shit. this is ridiculous.
mad maddie:	**so why don't u stop?**
zoegirl:	why don't U?
mad maddie:	**ok, i'm outta here**
zoegirl:	wait!
mad maddie:	**what?**
zoegirl:	thank u. i DO mean it.
zoegirl:	it's just that u must think i'm so pathetic.
mad maddie:	**i'm listening**
zoegirl:	cuz . . . u know. cuz it was all so awful. cuz i was, like, paralyzed, just sitting there clenching my toes while mr. h kept inching his way toward me. u'd never have let something like that happen.
mad maddie:	**uh, no, i'd just whip off my shirt instead. IF there were a hundred drunk frat boys there to appreciate it.**
zoegirl:	oh, god
zoegirl:	what is WRONG with us?
mad maddie:	**i have no idea**
zoegirl:	i am so embarrassed
mad maddie:	**well join the club**
zoegirl:	i know. maybe i need a little bit of u—like your "screw u" ballsiness—and u need a little bit of me, like my lame-o scaredy-cat-ness. only in a good way (if that is possible).
mad maddie:	**ur not a lame-o scaredy-cat.**
zoegirl:	oh yeah?
mad maddie:	**well, maybe last nite u were.**

Send   Cancel

mad maddie:	**but unlike me, u never would have screwed up so royally at that frat party. and NOT cuz u would have been scared, but just cuz u don't get sucked in by the whole popularity game. which is great. don't get me wrong, but it's one of the reasons i felt so stupid about what happened. cuz i knew u were thinking u were so much better than me.**
zoegirl:	well, i wasn't. we all make mistakes—obviously.
mad maddie:	**maybe**
zoegirl:	why wouldn't u talk to us about it? we were totally there for u, but it's like u didn't want us.
mad maddie:	**i DIDN'T, at first, cuz i was so pissed. and then the more time that went by, the harder it got. it just sucked, basically.**
zoegirl:	it sucked for us 2
zoegirl:	and i know i already told u this, but i AM sorry that angela and i talked behind your back. but honestly, we didn't mean to.
mad maddie:	**i know. i'm sorry for being such a freak.**
zoegirl:	and i'm sorry for not being a better friend, or whatever.
mad maddie:	**should we like be playing violins and shit? angela would be bawling her eyes out.**
zoegirl:	and ur not? jk
mad maddie:	**speaking of angela, what would we throw in from her? if we were creating the perfect mix of the 3 of us, that is.**
zoegirl:	i don't know. her love of makeup?
mad maddie:	**her love of boys?**
zoegirl:	her love of US? *ooo, group hug! group hug!*
mad maddie:	**ZOE! i can't believe u said that!**

Send   Cancel

zoegirl:	c? i'm not such a saint.
mad maddie:	**i'd say u proved that last nite, sister.**
zoegirl:	ack. oh, i don't wanna think about it.
zoegirl:	i'm just teasing about angela, tho. u know i love her.
mad maddie:	**and u know i do 2. *big sloppy kiss***
zoegirl:	and fine, i admit it. it was pretty awesome when u 2 showed up last nite.
mad maddie:	**for real?**
zoegirl:	how u strolled thru the kravitzes' back gate, gabbing about what a fabulous nite it was for hot-tubbing? and when u dropped down b/w us, stretching out your legs and taking up as much room as possible? i about died.
mad maddie:	**just doing my duty, ma'am**
zoegirl:	omg, u were practically in his lap.
mad maddie:	**AND he was wearing a speedo, which made it doubly horrific.**
mad maddie:	**shit, zoe, what r u gonna do when u c him on monday?!!**
zoegirl:	i have no idea
mad maddie:	**what is HE gonna do?**
zoegirl:	god, i seriously have no idea
zoegirl:	it pretty much makes me sick to even think about. i wish i could switch out of his class, but i know it's impossible.
mad maddie:	**couldn't u get your mom to request it?**
zoegirl:	and tell her WHAT?
mad maddie:	**ooo. good point.**
mad maddie:	**at least u won't have to waste your time with that religious crap anymore.**
zoegirl:	it wasn't the church's fault, tho. i LIKED the church.

Send   Cancel

mad maddie:	**oh, lord**
zoegirl:	but i'm not worried about that. i'm worried about HIM.
mad maddie:	**well, we'll figure something out together, u and me and angela. cuz, u know, all 3 of us r such pros when it comes to guys.**
zoegirl:	lord have mercy
zoegirl:	so . . . whatever happened with ian? did u straighten things out with him?
mad maddie:	**i've only seen him once since halloween, and that was last saturday when we worked together. at first he was all aloof, but we were thrown together so much that it was pretty much impossible NOT to talk.**
zoegirl:	r u 2 a thing again, then?
mad maddie:	**i wouldn't say we're a "thing." i'd say we're a "maybe." i didn't tell him exactly what happened that nite, but he knows i ditched him for jana, and he wasn't exactly thrilled.**
zoegirl:	i can c that, i guess
zoegirl:	what about jana? r u guys gonna patch things up?
mad maddie:	**u have to ASK?**
mad maddie:	**u and angela were right—jana's a bitch. case closed.**
zoegirl:	oh. well, sorry.
mad maddie:	**let's drop it, ok? she's not worth talking about.**
zoegirl:	ur so right
zoegirl:	well, here's a thought. if things work out with u and ian, then u 2 could double-date with angela and doug. (hee, hee)

Send   Cancel

mad maddie:	**angela and doug? as in doug schmidt?**
zoegirl:	the one and only
mad maddie:	**what happened to the schlank-master?**
zoegirl:	geez, ur behind the times. this is what u get when u drop off the face of the earth for 2 weeks.
mad maddie:	**fine, i guess i deserved that.**
zoegirl:	angela saw doug at a poetry slam—he read a poem about dirty underwear—and i guess they had a really good convo. she CLAIMS she's not gonna start crushing on him, but u know angela.
mad maddie:	**good grief. will the madness ever stop?**
mad maddie:	**GOD it's good to talk to u. seriously, the last 2 weeks have been hell. it's like without u and angela, i didn't know who i was anymore.**
zoegirl:	ur maddie, that's who. madigan kinnick, who swoops in like wonder woman to rescue me from sex-crazed english teachers. and who thinks up terrific ideas that angela or i would never come up with, like taking a road trip to cumberland island. r we still on?
mad maddie:	**u mean u still want to?**
zoegirl:	of course, ya goof
mad maddie:	**what about your parents?**
zoegirl:	what about them? as far as they know, the trip was never off. is that a problem?
mad maddie:	**no! it's just that i never thought**
mad maddie:	**i mean, i just assumed**
zoegirl:	what, that angela and i would let u bail on what's bound to be the most exciting thanksgiving vacation of our lives?

mad maddie:	**ah, crap. now i really am getting teary, can u believe it? i can't freakin believe i'm getting teary over this.**
zoegirl:	then we have GOT to call angela. she would kill us if she missed this historic moment.
mad maddie:	**crap again! angela! i'm supposed to pick her up so we can go to shoney's breakfast bar!**
zoegirl:	who's "we"?
mad maddie:	**!!!**
mad maddie:	**all 3 of us, of course**
zoegirl:	ohhhh.
zoegirl:	only i can't! shit! mom came up earlier and wanted me to go run some errands with her, and i told her i had a headache!
mad maddie:	**so?**
zoegirl:	so what am i supposed to do, tell her i've miraculously recovered now that it's u guys who r asking me to do something?
mad maddie:	**works for me**
zoegirl:	but what if she realized i'd been lying and it made her wonder what ELSE i've been lying about and . . . and . . .
zoegirl:	oh screw it. works for me 2.
mad maddie:	**for real? wh-hoo!**
zoegirl:	does this mean things r good b/w us again?!
mad maddie:	**totally**
zoegirl:	yay. i'm glad.
mad maddie:	**it's funny how some things r easier to talk about over the computer, isn't it?**

Send   Cancel

zoegirl: but other things—like our road trip—r much more exciting to talk about in person. so get off your butt and come get me!

mad maddie: right on. to shoney's, my comrade!

zoegirl: talk to u soon!!!

Send   Cancel

About the Author

Unlike many, Lauren Myracle remembers high school with fondness. She says, "When I was a sophomore, I had three especially great friends: Julianne, Maggie, and Gini. We did everything together. But for some reason, people liked to tell us (in that way that pretends to be nice but really isn't) to enjoy it while we could, because high school friendships never last. That was the idea I wanted to explore when I wrote *ttyl.* Because why do people assume that high school friendships aren't as real and enduring as other friendships? We all get to choose what kind of friend to be, no matter our age."

Ms. Myracle holds an MFA in Writing for Children and Young Adults from Vermont College. She lives in Colorado with her husband, Jack, and her sons Al and Jamie. She doesn't use instant messaging to keep up with Julianne, Maggie, and Gini, but she e-mails them frequently.

And they always respond.

This book was designed by Steve Kennedy and art directed by Becky Terhune. The text was set in 10-point Georgia, The Sans 9-Black, and Comic Sans.

Enjoy this peek at the second book in Lauren Myracle's
New York Times bestselling *Internet Girls* series

t t f n

(ta-ta for now)

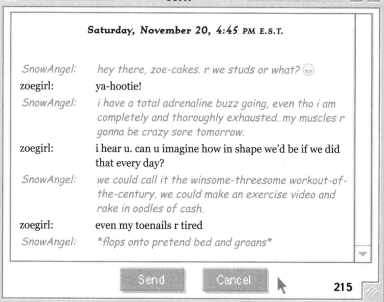

	ttfn	

Saturday, November 20, 4:45 PM E.S.T.

SnowAngel:	hey there, zoe-cakes. r we studs or what?
zoegirl:	ya-hootie!
SnowAngel:	i have a total adrenaline buzz going, even tho i am completely and thoroughly exhausted. my muscles r gonna be crazy sore tomorrow.
zoegirl:	i hear u. can u imagine how in shape we'd be if we did that every day?
SnowAngel:	we could call it the winsome-threesome workout-of-the-century. we could make an exercise video and rake in oodles of cash.
zoegirl:	even my toenails r tired
SnowAngel:	*flops onto pretend bed and groans*

Send   Cancel

SnowAngel:	i told chrissy what we did, and she was like, "u ran up the escalator at peachtree center? that super duper long one?"
zoegirl:	the critical point is that we ran up the *down* escalator. u did explain that to her, didn't u?
zoegirl:	that's gotta be the longest escalator in the world. seriously, it's as long as a football field.
SnowAngel:	i nearly lost it when maddie stopped for a breather and the escalator took her down, down, down. she was all, "noooo! i'm losing ground!"
zoegirl:	hee hee
SnowAngel:	but in the end we conquered it, cuz we can conquer ANYTHING, baby.
SnowAngel:	it's like my new favorite song, "run" by snow patrol. it goes, "light up, light up, as if u have a choice," and it's all about not giving into the harshness of life even when everything's going against u.
zoegirl:	"as if u have a choice"? sounds sarcastic.
SnowAngel:	no, no, no, it's not. have u heard it?
zoegirl:	is this another of those indie bands u discovered on your "OC" cd?
SnowAngel:	i discovered this one on my own, thank u very much. *pokes out tongue* the song is all melancholy and wistful, but at the same time beautiful and inspiring, and the lead singer's NOT being sarcastic. he's saying, "yeah, the world is hard, and maybe we don't have control, but we should ACT like we do. we should light up inside ourselves and shine."
SnowAngel:	i thoroughly agree, that's all.
zoegirl:	well i do 2
SnowAngel:	and the REASON i shine is cuz of u and mads. ☺☺☺
zoegirl:	awwwww

Send   Cancel

SnowAngel:	it's true. true blue, me and u, and don't forget to add maddie 2.
SnowAngel:	do u like my rhyme?
zoegirl:	very impressive
SnowAngel:	wait, there's more! er, let's c . . . since 7th grade they did not part, they stayed connected in their hearts. zoe's the good girl, maddie's wild, and sweet darling angela is meek and mild.
zoegirl:	meek? hahahahaha! mild? hahahahaha!
SnowAngel:	fine, miss brainiac. U find something to rhyme with wild.
zoegirl:	"and sweet goofy angela tends to act like a child"?
SnowAngel:	hey now!
zoegirl:	just teasing. u know i love u.
zoegirl:	i've just got kid-type ppl on my brain, cuz guess what? i got the job at Kidding Around!
SnowAngel:	wh-hoo! *happy dance, happy dance*
zoegirl:	there was a message waiting for me when i got home. i'm psyched.
SnowAngel:	ah, to be wiping noses and chasing toddlers. when do u start?
zoegirl:	um, don't freak, ok?
SnowAngel:	why would i freak? ur not gonna say something to make me freak, r u?
SnowAngel:	wait a minute. don't u DARE tell me u have to start tonite.
zoegirl:	the thing is . . . i do.
SnowAngel:	zoe! noooo!
zoegirl:	saturday nite's their busiest nite. the director wants me to come in for training.
SnowAngel:	but we were gonna watch "A Cinderella Story"! we were gonna freeze-frame the part where Hilary

Send   Cancel

	Duff goes into the locker room and has a fight with Chad Michael Murray!
zoegirl:	i know, and i will miss chad very much and pray that he understands. but we can have our "cinderella story" extravaganza tomorrow. that'll be even better, cuz that way maddie can actually join us.
SnowAngel:	the point being that she has plans tonite 2? yeah, rub it in. u've got ur job and maddie has her cousin's wedding and i have a big old pile of poop. thanks a lot.
zoegirl:	angela, u r such a drama queen.
SnowAngel:	😩
zoegirl:	ur not really mad, r u?
SnowAngel:	of course i'm mad! *flames shoot from ears*
SnowAngel:	only not really, cuz this way i can watch "extreme makeover: home edition" and no one will be here to make fun of me. and i will cry and it will be very emotional, and if u would just TRY the show then u would c what i mean.
zoegirl:	umm . . . no
zoegirl:	but u know what's weird? and i mean this in the nicest way ever. last year u would have been totally upset if i'd changed our plans at the last minute. i mean, truly upset, with all kinds of wounded hurt feelings. but this year, ur so much more chill. why is that, do u think?
SnowAngel:	cuz i'm a junior, that's why. *struts around in funky junior-ness* cuz i can drive, even tho i don't have a car. cuz i choose to light up, light up, even tho i will be all alone on a saturday nite, and even tho there is seriously something up with my parents, not that they'll admit it.
zoegirl:	there's something up with your parents? explain.
SnowAngel:	it's just this feeling i've been getting.

Send   Cancel

zoegirl:	like what? and for how long?
SnowAngel:	i dunno, maybe a week?
zoegirl:	a week?! why r u just now telling me???
SnowAngel:	it's like they're hiding something, i can't explain it better than that. i keep thinking that maybe i'm making it up, but then i think that i'm not.
zoegirl:	hmm, interesting
zoegirl:	maybe it's a *good* thing they're hiding—like, that they're taking u to hawaii.
SnowAngel:	i dunno, that somehow doesn't seem very likely.
SnowAngel:	but, whatever. i'm not gonna worry about it, cuz i'm the new and improved Chill Angela. u think they would name a Barbie after me?
zoegirl:	definitely. and for the accessory, she could have a tiny iPod so she could listen to that "light up" song.
SnowAngel:	no, her accessory would be a tiny picture of u, me, and mads, cuz that's why i'm chill for real. cuz no matter what, i've got u guys giving me my me-ness. ☺
zoegirl:	maddie and i don't give u ur you-ness. u give urself ur you-ness.
SnowAngel:	"you-ness." now there's a word for u.
SnowAngel:	my granddad's name was eunice, btw
zoegirl:	grandDAD? u mean ur grandmom.
SnowAngel:	nope, my granddad. only he spelled it "unus."
zoegirl:	ugh. what were his parents trying to do to him?
SnowAngel:	his full name was unus faye. he went by U.F.
zoegirl:	i am so sorry to hear that.
SnowAngel	yep
zoegirl:	well, on that note, gtg. wish me luck on my first day, which is really my first nite!
SnowAngel:	good luck on ur first day which is really ur first nite!
SnowAngel:	ta ta for now!

Send   Cancel

Saturday, November 20, 5:16 PM E.S.T.

SnowAngel:	hey, maderoo. getting all dolled up for ur cousin's wedding?
mad maddie:	**fyi, the dolling is done. fyi, i look fabu.**
mad maddie:	**the pops, however, has hit a new low.**
SnowAngel:	ooo, do tell
mad maddie:	**ahem. he bought this self-hair-cutter thing, right? cuz he's such a cheapskate that he didn't wanna fork over 10 bucks at lloyd's barbershop. and of course he decides that today, the day of donovan's wedding, is the perfect day for a trim. so i get home to find dad in the bathroom, hair-cutter aloft, and as i walk to my room, i hear the buzzing begin. bzzzzzzzzzzzzz.**
SnowAngel:	what'd he do, give himself a mohawk?
mad maddie:	**if only. so then the buzzing stops, and he goes, "oops." "what happened?" i yell. and he says, "i put on the wrong attachment. guess my hair will be a little shorter than usual, huh?"**
SnowAngel:	uh oh
mad maddie:	**and then for some reason he starts asking if i have a safety pin or a needle or anything pokey. i think he was taking the whole thing apart. but no, i did not have anything pokey, so after a while he puts it back together and the buzzing starts again. and then it shuts off. and he starts LAFFING.**
SnowAngel:	oh, crap. what happened?
mad maddie:	**my idiot father forgot to put ANY attachment back on, which meant that when he started up again, he took off an entire strip of hair down to his scalp. as in, bald. and then once he'd done that, he figured there was nothing to do but complete the scalping.**
mad maddie:	**my father is a cue ball, angela.**

Send   Cancel

SnowAngel:	oh no!
SnowAngel:	that cracks me up that he would laff, tho. that's so ur dad.
mad maddie:	**he was all, "what? it's just hair." the moms is massively annoyed.**
SnowAngel:	if my dad went bald on the day of a wedding, my mom would jump out a window. or push HIM out a window.
mad maddie:	**ah, well. we'll go to the reception and drink away our troubles, cuz that's what my family does. should be a good time.**
SnowAngel:	that blows my mind that u can drink right there with them.
mad maddie:	**it's cuz we're irish. it's the law.**
SnowAngel:	my parents would be like, "u r underage. go sit at the kiddie table." but yours r like, "here, have another beer!"
mad maddie:	**well, they won't be the ones actually giving me beers. they'll leave that to my crazy aunts and uncles. and it won't be beer, it'll be champagne.**
SnowAngel:	la di da
mad maddie:	**and before long uncle duncan will be ranting about the iraqis and aunt teresa will be doing the line dance she learned in 8th grade to michael jackson's "beat it."**
mad maddie:	**i'm telling u, donovan's fiancee has noooooo idea what she's in for.**
SnowAngel:	sounds fun, tho
mad maddie:	**it definitely won't be boring**
SnowAngel:	do u wish—even just a little—that u and ian were still going out, so he could go with u?
mad maddie:	**not at all. ian is a fleck and i am a plane, high in the sky. that's how over him i am.**

SnowAngel:	swear?
mad maddie:	**ok, maybe not a plane. maybe just a . . . telephone pole.**
SnowAngel:	meaning what?
mad maddie:	**meaning that maybe i do miss him, but what's the point? if ian had wanted to come to donovan's wedding with me, then he shouldn't have broken up with me.**
SnowAngel:	he didn't break up with u. u broke up with him.
mad maddie:	**but only cuz i knew that he was going to. he called me a ball and chain, if u don't recall.**
SnowAngel:	WHAT?!!
SnowAngel:	he did NOT call u a ball and chain. he made that ONE comment about wanting to hang out with his friends more, and u did your porcupine thing where u bristle up over nothing.
mad maddie:	**there was more to it than that 1 comment. it was obvious i was cramping his style.**
SnowAngel:	omg. only u would interpret it like that.
SnowAngel:	it's ok to have feelings, u know. it's even ok to miss ian.
mad maddie:	**thanx for that, Dr. Phil.**
SnowAngel:	he adored u, mads. he would take u back in a heartbeat.
mad maddie:	**yeah, well, that boat's already sailed.**
mad maddie:	**that's nice of u to say, tho. u r so good to me.**
SnowAngel:	yup, cuz i luv ya
SnowAngel:	anyway, who knows? maybe tonite u'll meet someone new. maybe u'll meet your future husband!
mad maddie:	**or maybe NOT. i'm not looking for a husband, angela— sheesh!**
SnowAngel:	u never know . . .
SnowAngel:	so zoe got that job at Kidding Around, did u hear?

Send   Cancel

mad maddie: that's such a dorky name, Kidding Around. it's like, "hiya, buddy, watcha up to?" "not much—just kidding around." with everyone slugging each other on the shoulder.

SnowAngel: cuz it's a childcare place, for when parents don't have a babysitter or whatever. KIDDING around. get it?

mad maddie: der, angela. not getting it was never the problem.

mad maddie: yikes, time to motor. old baldie's calling my name.

SnowAngel: have fun at the wedding! tell donovan congrats for me! OH, and u and zoe r both coming over tomorrow, ok? we're having Sunday Afternoon Movie Madness.

mad maddie: that sounds awesome—only not "A Cinderella Story." i am not watching u freeze-frame the locker room shot for the umpteenth billion time.

SnowAngel: we will take a vote

mad maddie: fine, we'll take a vote

SnowAngel: and my vote counts double since it's my house. ☺ buh-bye!

Saturday, November 20, 10:32 PM E.S.T.

mad maddie: dude! future hubby alert!

SnowAngel: for real???

mad maddie: no. cute boy, tho. very very cute.

SnowAngel: where r u? is the wedding over?

mad maddie: reception. boy's name = clive.

SnowAngel: CLIVE?

mad maddie: but i call him chive, cuz i = witty. friend of donovan.

SnowAngel: cool—i can't wait to hear more when ur not IMing from your cell. why r u, anyway? just call me!

mad maddie: can't. lurking behind dessert table.

SnowAngel:	maddie, get off the phone and go have fun. or else go somewhere and CALL me, cuz guess what? i think i figured out why my parents r being so weird.
mad maddie:	**spill**
SnowAngel:	it's zoe who helped me figure it out. she was all, "maybe what they're hiding is a GOOD thing, angela," and i think maybe she's right. i think they're buying me a car!
mad maddie:	**holy shit!**
SnowAngel:	i know!!! they keep talking in these hush-hush quiet voices, and then they clam up whenever i come in the room. it's extremely suspicious.
mad maddie:	**well, rock on**
mad maddie:	**as for me, it's bunny hop time!**

Sunday, November 21, 11:01 AM E.S.T.

zoegirl:	maddie! ur awake and it's only 11:00! how was the wedding?
mad maddie:	**it was awesome, altho i'm kinda hungover. not terrible, tho.**
zoegirl:	tell me more
mad maddie:	**it was mainly family, so the ceremony wasn't huge, but with my family that's probably a good thing. donovan looked great in his tux, and lisa looked drop-dead gorgeous.**
zoegirl:	yeah? what was her dress like?
mad maddie:	**her dress? i don't know. it was . . . white. NOT frou-frou. for lisa it was perfect, especially cuz she's so tiny. but like, naturally tiny. healthy tiny.**
zoegirl:	did she seem happy? was she glowing? when i fall in love, it's gonna be with someone who makes me glow.

Send   Cancel

mad maddie:	**ok, excuse me while i barf**
zoegirl:	whoa, u really r hungover
mad maddie:	**uh, no, i was barfing cuz somehow ur channeling angela with this "glowing" shit. why does everyone have to get all mushy when it comes to love?**
zoegirl:	i am *not* channeling angela. u cannot compare me to angela, that is so unfair.
mad maddie:	**i don't know if lisa was glowing, but she smiled a lot, and at the reception she gave me a big hug, which surprised me. i used to think she was snobby, but now i'm wondering if she's just shy.**
mad maddie:	**she's not, like, the coolest girl in the world, but she's the coolest girl for donovan, if that makes sense. i think they're good together.**
zoegirl:	well, that's awesome. u can be cynical maddie if u have to be, but i want that someday. i wanna fall in love for real.
mad maddie:	**u don't consider mr. h for real?**
zoegirl:	don't, maddie. i don't even like to joke about that.
mad maddie:	**about what? about the fact that u almost had an affair with your horny english teacher?**
zoegirl:	i am covering my ears now. la la la.
mad maddie:	**how about his whole christianity kick, can i joke about that? ya gotta admit, it's great material. it's not very often that a guy uses God to try and lure in the girls.**
zoegirl:	please stop
mad maddie:	**zo, it happened over a year ago. it's ancient history. when WILL i be allowed to joke about it?**
zoegirl:	*never*
zoegirl:	let's change the subject. i talked to angela this morning, and she said u met some guy named after a seasoning. cilantro? paprika?
mad maddie:	**ha ha. it's clive. i just call him chive. he goes to northside.**

zoegirl:	what grade's he in?
mad maddie:	**he's a junior. he loves music, which is why he goes to n'side since they have such a good performing arts department. i told him how i wanna major in music AND advertising and then be the person who makes CD covers.**
mad maddie:	**we talked forever—he's got GORGEOUS eyes—and then we ended up macking in the corner. the moms totally caught us, which believe me was completely embarrassing.**
zoegirl:	oh god
mad maddie:	**but she was wasted 2, so she didn't care. she got all teary and started saying stuff like, "u and clive! it's meant to be!" and i was like, "mom, no. i love being single." and she goes, "r u telling me ur a slut?"**
zoegirl:	nuh uh
mad maddie:	**then she calls out to all my aunts and uncles in this really loud voice, "someone bring me another drink— my little girl's a slut!"**
zoegirl:	i swear, maddie, your family is so incredibly different from mine. there is no way in the world i would ever have a convo like that with my mother.
mad maddie:	**cuz your family is normal**
mad maddie:	**she was just joking, tho. she was just being wild.**
zoegirl:	was chive around for all that? did he hear your mom call u a slut?
mad maddie:	**yeah, and he laffed. that's the cool thing about him.**
zoegirl:	huh
mad maddie:	**i had FUN, zo. the whole nite was fun. i know it's not your style, but i had a blast.**
zoegirl:	so r u gonna c him again?
mad maddie:	**who, chive? i hope so, yeah, but not in a date-y way if that's what ur asking.**
zoegirl:	why not in a date-y way, if u liked him so much?

Send   Cancel

mad maddie:	**cuz i'm not looking for that. we don't all have to GLOW, zo. we really don't.**
ad maddie:	**hey, how was your first nite at Kidding Around?**
zoegirl:	i *love* it. the kids r so cute. there was this one little boy, he was maybe 3, and he had all these fake tattoos on his arm. i would point to one and say, "so what's that?" and he'd say, "a snake, but not a *real* snake." or "a bat, but not a *real* bat." or "a lightning, but not a *real* lightning, cuz if it was real lightning, there would be thunder. only not here. somewhere else. where the indians r."
mad maddie:	**what indians?**
zoegirl:	beats me.
zoegirl:	oh—and guess who works there with me?!
mad maddie:	**who?**
zoegirl:	doug schmidt!
mad maddie:	**doug? as in angela's doug?**
zoegirl:	well, he's not really angela's doug, seeing as how she's not the slightest bit interested. but yeah. i was like, "doug! wow!"
mad maddie:	**he's gonna be all over u, i can c it now. he's gonna use u as an inside link. cuz angela may not be interested, but it's a sure bet he's still crushing on her.**
zoegirl:	maybe. i don't know. i just think it's cool that a guy would take a job there in the 1st place.
mad maddie:	**what'd angela say when u told her?**
zoegirl:	we didn't talk about it much, cuz she was kinda distracted. she thinks her parents r buying her a car.
mad maddie:	**oh yeah, that's right—and she says U planted the idea.**
zoegirl:	i did not! i just said she shouldn't assume that whatever's going on with her parents is bad.
zoegirl:	altho i may have to revise that opinion based on a new and not-so-good development. *don't* tell angela.

mad maddie:	**don't tell angela what?**
zoegirl:	i saw her dad at starbucks this morning. i was getting cappuccinos for my parents cuz i'm such a good daughter, and there was mr. silver. and he wasn't alone.
mad maddie:	**who was he with?**
zoegirl:	a woman, wearing a tailored skirt and blouse. the kind of woman who actually uses lip liner.
mad maddie:	**lip liner, that's hardcore.**
mad maddie:	**so what r u saying?**
zoegirl:	nothing, i'm not saying anything
mad maddie:	**u don't think he's having an affair, do u???**
zoegirl:	no no no, i'm sure he's not.
zoegirl:	i just got a weird vibe, that's all.
mad maddie:	**weird how?**
zoegirl:	u know how normally mr. silver's so friendly and buddy-buddy? well, today when i went over to say hi, he looked really uncomfortable. all brusque and at the same time blushing, like he'd been caught in the act.
mad maddie:	**WHAT act?**
zoegirl:	i dunno. and he didn't introduce me to the lip liner woman, even tho she was smiling very pleasantly like "oh, and who's your little friend?" it was 1 of those moments where he *should* have introduced us, but he didn't.
zoegirl:	there was something suspicious about it. it made me worry that
zoegirl:	never mind
mad maddie:	**what?**
zoegirl:	it's stupid. it's superstitious. but like, things r going *so well* for us. ur happy, angela's happy, i'm happy. and then i think, shit, when's the bad thing gonna happen, u know?

mad maddie:	**and u think the bad thing has to do with angela's dad and the lip liner woman?**
zoegirl:	i didn't say that
mad maddie:	**anywayz, ur crazy. enuff bad stuff happened to us last year to last a lifetime.**
zoegirl:	tell me about it. let's c, 1st there was me and mr. h, then angela and all her boy probs, and then as if that wasn't enuff, u went all psycho with your terrible jana obsession.
mad maddie:	**"obsession"? that's a bit of an exaggeration, wouldn't u say?**
zoegirl:	no. u were like her clone. u started to talk like her, dress like her . . .
zoegirl:	i am *so* glad ur over that, btw
mad maddie:	**listen, pal. if i'm not allowed to mention mr. h, then ur not allowed to bring up jana.**
zoegirl:	fine, then u know how i feel.
zoegirl:	but don't u c the pattern? it was last year right around thanksgiving that all hell broke loose, and now here we r, right around thanksgiving again.
mad maddie:	**nooooo, zoe. it was BEFORE last thanksgiving that all hell broke loose, cuz over thanksgiving itself, we were blissing out on cumberland island. or have u forgotten?**
zoegirl:	of course i haven't forgotten!
zoegirl:	why didn't we plan a trip for this year? weren't we gonna make it a tradition?
mad maddie:	**oops, 2 late now**
zoegirl:	c! that's what's making me feel this way. we're 2 complacent, just going along like everything's fine.
mad maddie:	**yeahhhh, cuz everything IS fine.**
mad maddie:	**don't worry, zo. life is good, and ain't nothin gonna change. c ya at angela's!**

Send   Cancel

Keep reading! If you liked this book, check out these other titles.

l8r, g8r
by Lauren Myracle
978-0-8109-1266-3 $15.95 hardcover
978-0-8109-7086-1 $6.95 paperback

ttfn
by Lauren Myracle
978-0-8109-5971-2 $15.95 hardcover
978-0-8109-9279-5 $6.95 paperback

Rhymes with Witches
by Lauren Myracle
978-0-8109-5859-3 $16.95 hardcover
978-0-8109-9215-3 $6.95 paperback

Keep reading! If you liked this book, check out these other titles.

Something to Blog About
By Shana Norris
978-0-8109-9474-4 $15.95 hardcover

Fell
By David Clement-Davies
978-0-8109-1185-7 $19.95 hardcover

Such a Pretty Face:
Short Stories About Beauty
Edited by Ann Angel
978-0-8109-1607-4 $18.95 hardcover

Visit www.amuletbooks.com to download screen savers and ring tones, to find out where authors will be appearing, and to send e-cards.

AVAILABLE WHEREVER BOOKS ARE SOLD

Send author fan mail to Amulet Books, Attn: Marketing, 115 West 18th Street, New York, NY 10011 or in an e-mail to *marketing@hnabooks.com*. All mail will be forwarded. Amulet Books is an imprint of Harry N. Abrams, Inc.